ELLE STOCKTON

BOURBON STREET NOCTURNE

and Other

SHORT STORIES

Fictional tales on a ride of twists, turns, and the unexpected

This book is a work of fiction. Any references to historical events, real people, or real locales are used fictitiously. Other names, characters, places, and incidents are the product of the author's imagination, and any resemblance to actual events or locales or persons, living or dead is entirely coincidental.

Printed by Kindle Direct Publishing, An Amazon.com Company
Available from Amazon.com and other online stores
Available on Kindle and other devices.

ISBN: 978-0-578-89712-7

Library of Congress Control Number: 2021906122

PRINTED IN THE UNITED STATES OF AMERICA

Also by Elle Stockton

Harvest Moon Wish and Other Short Stories
Fictional tales on a ride of twists, turns, and the unexpected

To Maleko (Mark) Hirshfeld

Nani Kane Male Hou

Acknowledgments

Thank you for making my vision a reality!
Consulting, Mark A. Hirshfeld
Cover Design and Illustration, Rafael Andrés
Editor, Jessica McKelden
Interior Design, Rafael Andrés

Contents

INTRODUCTION

Welcome to *Bourbon Street Nocturne and Other Short Stories: Fictional tales on a ride of twists, turns, and the unexpected,* the second book in my series of fictional stories. If you have read the first book, *Harvest Moon Wish and Other Short Stories: Fictional tales on a ride of twists, turns, and the unexpected,* you will find a significant genre that has been added to this collection—noir. For my entire life, I've read hardboiled detective stories with the femme fatales they crave, and just had to add this sassy genre to my new book.

Prepare to be frightened, fascinated, mystified, and romanced as you immerse yourself in the tales of this multigenre book—dark fantasy, horror, murder mystery, noir, romance, suspense, psychological thriller, and humor.

You may laugh frequently and cry at least once. I cried my guts out when I finished typing the last two paragraphs of one particular story. The cohesive thread throughout these tales is the twist of fate experienced by the characters.

Your challenge, dear reader, is to figure out the twist before it happens.

As an author, my job is to present to you the gift of discovery in sorting out colorful characters with their conflicts and the worlds around them.

Hence, onward into a labyrinth of sixty compelling stories with intertwists that will hold you in their grip from beginning to end. I sincerely hope you have as much enjoyment reading the stories as I had writing them. Thank you for joining me.

—Elle Stockton, a.k.a. Robin B. Stockton

SOMETHING WAS NOT RIGHT

Rosemary had an eerie feeling that something was not right. She was exhausted, and her eyes were shut tight while she tried to sleep. However, she couldn't shake the feeling that someone was with her.

She rested comfortably in her favorite nighttime conditions—darkness and a cool temperature. She stretched out in her preferred position—on her back. Her head was well supported by a silk pillow. Her arms lay on each side of her body in a relaxed, meditative pose.

Rosemary dreamed that a handsome, gray-haired gentleman took her into his arms and kissed her deeply. Their passion heightened with each kiss until he carried her into the bedroom and made love to her without stopping. They were caught up in an ecstatic world of their own that neither of them had experienced before.

Was he the person who was still with Rosemary?

Neither of them noticed an older woman entering the room. In a fog, Rosemary vaguely recognized her as someone who worked for her beloved. The woman held a gun on Rosemary, while she injected the gentleman with a drug that knocked him out.

Rosemary's restlessness stirred as she heard something in the distance. It was a vaguely familiar sound. Her eyes shot open with a start.

Her hands felt the tight confinement of a wooden box. The sound moved closer to her.

Thump, thump. It started slowly, then increased in rapidity. It reverberated loudly in the box, an echo chamber of death.

What Rosemary heard was the beating of her own heart. Her lover's ex-wife had buried her alive.

A RAINY DAY IN KENSINGTON

"Fancy a cuppa?" asked a drab-uniformed tea server.

"Sencha green tea," answered a fashionably-dressed woman wrapped in a cashmere-belted overcoat and matching scarf. She removed her compact mirror with lipstick holder attached and applied Coco Chanel's signature red lipstick to her pristine lips. Satisfied with her attractive, forty-year-old visage, she slipped the compact into her purse and looked through the window at the gently falling rain.

The woman didn't seem to notice when her tea appeared. She bit into a macaron and swallowed her tea. Before she could even finish chewing her cookie, she fell off her chair onto the floor and began convulsing, foam pouring from her mouth. Then she stopped moving.

Inspector Smythe sniffed the cup of tea and remarked, "I smell licorice. Please bag the cup and have it checked out by toxicology." He used a napkin to hand it to a detective. "Could have been someone added absinthe with toxic wormwood to the tea. Where is her tea server?"

The young server was knitting a light blue baby blanket over the small bump in her stomach while sitting next to her comatose husband in a hospital. The deceased woman had struck him with her fashionable car and fled two weeks earlier. She had been touching up her lipstick in the rearview mirror while driving.

DARKEST DESIRE

Julian yearned for the burning passion of a woman in his life. He longed for a sophisticated, stylish female who would satiate his appetite for an array of dark sexual desires. Bored with traditional dating, he bought a ticket for a dining-in-the-dark sensory experience.

The evening in Hollywood arrived. Once Julian stepped out of an elevator, he was immediately blindfolded by a red silk sash, which a gentleman tied with a knot at the back of his head. The waiter escorted Julian to a dark dining room and helped him into a plush chair. Julian heard chatter across the table.

Suddenly, he felt long fingernails lightly stroke the sleeve of his woolen jacket, then rest with a feminine hand on his right thigh. He heard the swish of silk from the female in the chair to his right as she moved closer to him. Her perfume exhilarated his senses. Julian reached out and felt the silky, smooth bare skin of her back, stroked it, then wrapped his hand around her neck for a moment.

"I'm Mara," she said.

"Julian, here," he responded. "Your scent is intoxicating."

"I'm wearing my favorite rose—Dark Desire," she said in a low voice.

"Exactly what I'm looking for," Julian whispered.

The sound of plates being placed on the table, and the aroma of fresh bread, cinnamon, and exotic spices pervaded the room.

"You know, we're eating with our hands tonight," Mara said.

"Yes. I can't wait to taste the bread," Julian responded.

Julian felt around in the dark and touched a large basket, raised it, and brought it closer to him. He carefully removed a large piece, took a bite, and said, "Moroccan bread. We can use the bread in place of utensils tonight. Have you eaten Moroccan before, Mara?" he asked.

"Yes, Julian," she answered.

"How enticing," he said.

Julian felt for the plate and bent over it. He pushed the bread, sliding mouthful portions of couscous and vegetables together and used it with his fingers to scoop the food into his mouth. It was a painstakingly slow process.

Julian slumped over his dish. The rest of the group was busily banging their dishes while eating, talking, and laughing in the dark. Except for Mara.

After the dinner ended, the staff found that Mara's plate of food remained untouched. No one saw her leave—or enter for that matter. However, a prickly rose rested on the seat of her chair, and a small window high above it was left ajar.

A DISH WELL SERVED

She was a hot dish with a juicy, blood-rare steak and two loaded potatoes, ready for dinner. The tomato taunted him with it, and, after two shots of whiskey, he was ready to bite. He grabbed her by the shoulders and kissed her hard on her sumptuous lips.

"This is what you've been waiting for, baby," he said to her.

When she pulled away, he pressed her against his chest and kissed her deeply. "I bet you haven't been kissed like that for a long time," he said.

"A girl has to come up for air," she said. Then she turned away from him and gulped down a glass of water.

“If you can’t take the heat, get out of the kitchen, honey,” he said to her.

She paid her tab. Then she stood up, put on a coat, grabbed her purse, and responded, “You shouldn’t play with fire, baby. You might get burned.”

He started to stand up, and she rushed out of the dive into the mist.

He ordered another shot to cap off the evening. After he let the whiskey wash it all down, he reached into the pocket of a jacket for his wallet. It wasn’t there.

The dish had gotten it right. He shouldn’t have played with fire.

HOME COOKING

Gallagher stared at her caboose. *She's a looker,* he thought to himself.

He returned a few phone calls with the image of the sexy redhead in her tight black dress and high heels fresh on his mind. He couldn't shake her off. Gallagher was in—hook, line, and sinker.

On his drive home, he replayed her shimmy out the door in his head. *She knows how to use it all right.* He smiled to himself.

Gallagher opened the door to a dark home. He put his briefcase down, then walked through a dark hallway and into the dining room enhanced by candlelight. He sat down at the table.

The aroma of tomato and herbs filled the room. A plate of lasagna was placed before him. "I thought we would eat in tonight, honey," his wife said.

He grinned, grabbed her around the waist, and planted a big one on her kisser.

"They always say home cooking is best," the sexy redhead said while she poured a glass of cabernet for her husband.

BLIND DATE: IT WASN'T HER

"C'mon, let's go," she said.

It wasn't her flashy black coupe. It wasn't her long, dark hair and large, dark eyes. It wasn't her pretty, summery dress.

Her blind date did a double take. He spun around twice, struck by Cupid's arrow.

It was her sweet, sweet smile.

BLACK BEARS

After her parents' estate was settled, and Faye had their Colonial mansion, stocks, bonds, and liquid assets all to herself, she became easy prey for con artists who wanted a piece of the action. At the age of fifty, Faye was pretty, stylish, and available. She was dark haired, light amber-eyed, and had the figure of a female half her age.

One might wonder why Faye had not married. Though she had been in a few red-hot relationships, they were always short-lived, ending in furious breakups. She had a temper the likes of which no earthly human would seek to encounter.

Living alone in her parents' twelve-thousand-square-foot, five-acre estate, Faye was lonely. Out in the isolated mountains of Anderson, North Carolina, there were no neighbors nearby to have a chat. Only large black bears and pesky mosquitoes kept Faye's company.

She decided a luxury Caribbean cruise would improve her social life, so Faye booked it on the Internet. Her cabin was small, but filled with basic necessities. On her first night, Faye had the pleasure of dining at the captain's table. While the other guests stared at her flowing, silver-beaded gown, Faye had her eyes set on a tan, dark, handsome man in a black tuxedo seated across the table from her. She couldn't stop staring at him.

He asked her to dance, and they looked attractive together. Arturo asked Faye for a stroll on the deck afterward, and she accepted. After spending several steamy days and smoldering nights with Arturo, Faye felt like she had known him her entire life. She was in love for the first time in twenty years. As usual, Faye's feelings always came first in her life.

She felt certain that Arturo was going to ask her to marry him and looked forward to their last evening on the cruise. Arturo had gone ashore to shop, while Faye stayed onboard to calm her nerves. As she turned the corner by the ship's incoming telegrams, she peeked in and read a message for her love.

"Arturo, your wife is in labor. Hurry home. From TriStar Hendersonville Medical Center, North Carolina."

Every muscle in Faye's body tightened and she started shaking from head to foot. The ship's captain found her in distress and helped Faye back to her room. She packed her bags, poured a large glass of water, and took an Ativan and two sleeping pills.

Faye never heard Arturo knock repeatedly on her door that evening. She slept soundly, awoke with a firm resolve, and left her room when the ship docked. Her butler came aboard to collect her bags, and she walked off with her head held high.

Faye knew that she had narrowly escaped the claws of the worst kind of predator. She much preferred the black bears of North Carolina.

OUT OF OPTIONS

"I'm your mother," she pleaded with her son, Reilly.

"I want fifty dollars and I want it now," he demanded, pointing a gun at her stomach.

Marissa had been through this same sad scenario with her drug-addicted son several times during the past five years. Drug rehabilitation and jail had only made Reilly meaner and more difficult to be around. Marissa had no options left.

"Then shoot. I am not going to help you throw your life away," she said firmly.

"Come on, Mom. I have no one else left," he whined.

"Isn't that my point?" asked his mom.

Reilly dropped the gun to the floor and fell into his mother's arms, sobbing.

HER MIND'S EYE

In her mind's eye, Tara's seventeen-year-old long, slender legs propelled her through the air, where she flew high above the other ballerinas.

Plié, demi-plié, and bend. Pirouette, she thought, as she imagined herself working gracefully on the dance floor. She seemed to float in a set of three triple pirouette turns. Then she finished her ballet recital with four masterful split leaps diagonally across the floor.

Tara turned her head and smiled at the ballerina in the jewelry box next to the bed where she had been napping.

DELLA DANWORTH, PRIVATE DETECTIVE

Clip, clip, clip. The sound of Della Danworth's high heels hitting the sidewalk bounced back and forth between the tall cement buildings in Manhattan until she reached the residential apartment building of *The Pierre.* She headed straight to the elevator, up to the ninth floor, and rang the bell of Mrs. Phyllis Carlyle's residence, which occupied the entire floor.

"She's waiting for you in the drawing room," said the maid who answered the door, and led Della to Phyllis.

"Nine o'clock in the morning and you are right on the dot. I like punctuality in my employees," Phyllis said, a pen and notebook in hand.

"Mrs. Carlyle, let's not get ahead of ourselves," Della said. "You told my secretary that you had a delicate situation and needed my detective services. I am here. Now, what can I do for you?" asked Della.

"You don't mince words. All right, then. My only daughter, Pauline, has been missing for two days and the police won't do anything about it. She is seventeen years old and has been in trouble before, which I settled out of court. They believe she has run away," said Phyllis.

"Well, has she?" asked Della.

"Of course not. She doesn't come into her trust fund until she turns twenty-five. However, I determine whether or not she is fiscally responsible enough to manage the money her father put aside for her. Until then, I am her guardian," Phyllis answered.

"What kind of trouble has she been in?" asked Della.

"The wrong type of boys with fast cars," answered Phyllis. "The last time, her girlfriend had her right arm maimed in a bad accident. I had to pay the parents off. It will be a miracle if I see my girl graduate from high school. Then I'm sending her off to an all-female college in St. Louis, Missouri."

"I'll need a small photograph and a contact list of her friends, boyfriends, and high school teachers and counselor. I charge ten dollars a day plus expenses," said Della.

"That will be fine. You may talk to anybody you want, but not those settled out of court. I'll have my attorney send you over a list," Phyllis responded.

"I'll be in touch when I learn something," Della said, and left.

Della hailed a hack and told the driver to go to the Crayton Academy for Girls. She went to the principal's office and learned that Miss Ellington was out for the afternoon. Instead, she met with Mr. Farthington, Pauline's counselor, a handsome man in his mid-thirties. Pauline's counselor found her to be an intelligent and engaging young female and had no idea why she wasn't in school. Her other teachers said that she performed well in their classes, was friendly with the other students, and couldn't imagine why she wasn't in school.

Della decided that the Crayton Academy for Girls did not allow problems to exist—and would not admit them if they did.

Della took a taxi back to her office and found the list she'd requested in an envelope from Mrs. Carlyle on her desk. She lit a cigarette and started to think. There was something about Crayton Academy that seemed off. She pulled Pauline's photograph from the envelope and studied it. She looked mature for her age—almost eighteen—and gorgeous.

Della knew when she had a hunch, she was usually right. She stuffed the contents back into the envelope, locked the office, ran downstairs, and hailed another cab. She pulled out the list and asked the driver to take her to upstate New York where they were going to stake out a suspect. The driver said it was her two bits.

Della dozed while the driver drove, then awoke when he started to slow down. The address belonged to a small cabin with a view of a lake. She told the driver to park off the road, near the pine trees. It was the golden hour, the reflection of the sun shining down on the lake. Della also made out the sunlight on Pauline, who was coming out of the water from a swim.

Walking toward her with a towel to dry her off was Mr. Farthington!

Della told the driver to pull over to Pauline. She opened her car door, stood her full six-foot frame in front of Pauline, and asked, "Should I drive you home or do you want me to call your mother?"

NEEDLE AND THREAD

She was born before her time during the last decade of the nineteenth century in New York. Women were supposed to wear frilly long dresses, marry well, and breed. Lauren Langley, on the other hand, wore knee-high black boots, sensible long skirts, neck-high shirts with men's ties, jackets, and her signature black wool top hat.

Lauren had studied nursing and refined her skills surgically on soldiers who returned home from war overseas with bullet wounds or limbs that needed amputation, prosthesis, and rehabilitation. Lauren proved that a needle and thread could be used by a woman to do more than embellish ballroom gowns for frivolous parties. She walked with confidence, used the precision of words to get to the point, and could be counted on in difficult situations.

Young girls in a fragile state without means called upon Lauren to deliver their babies they'd conceived out of wedlock, and bring them to respectable agencies for placement with responsible married couples—no questions asked. Lauren noticed that most of these girls were too young to willingly bear pregnancy. They were children who had been sexually assaulted by men who'd wielded power over them.

These girls served the wealthiest families in New York by performing jobs that only the less fortunate would do. Washing and drying clothes, scrubbing floors, polishing silver, dusting, changing dirty linens, drawing baths, mending torn clothes—the list of tasks to keep wealthy households going was endless. In exchange for their labor, they received a few coins, the back of a hand, and unwanted attention from men who thought of them as property.

Lauren had seen her share of young girls dumped in back alleys like trash with nowhere to go. Wives of bankers, brokers, and the privileged simply accepted what their husbands did to the girls and ordered their drivers to dump them once they started to show a bump in the belly. The wives were no better than the husbands who had raped these girls.

Eliza, the twelve-year-old daughter of Irish Catholic immigrants, was disowned by her family once she began to show. A newspaper tycoon had returned home early one day, found his wife out playing cards with her friends, and had taken advantage of Eliza in a broom closet.

Lauren found Eliza sobbing in an alley next to the market, with nowhere to go. She took Eliza to live with her in a modest apartment during the pregnancy.

Lauren helped Eliza through her delivery of two healthy infant sons. She repaired Eliza's vaginal tears with a needle and thread. Eliza and her sons stayed on with Lauren and they became a happy family.

Eliza spent her time taking care of the boys, cooking, and cleaning the apartment. When the boys turned one year old, Eliza knitted their names in red yarn on white sweaters.

On a Sunday morning in the park while pushing the boys in their carriages, a woman stopped to look at them. "My husband's name is John and his brother's name is James. They even look like both of them," she remarked in awe. "I never had any children," she said. The newspaper magnate's wife overlooked Eliza, just as she had when the young female had worked inside her mansion.

"It must be their sweaters. It's amazing what a needle and thread can do," Lauren responded, as she and Eliza quickly pushed the carriages away from the boys' birth father's wife.

Lauren's needle and thread had repaired the lives of broken soldiers and pregnant young girls, and skillfully fabricated a family of her own.

SOLE MATE

As far back as Tilly could remember, her feet were always in the way. Falls from nursery school through high school left her knees scarred from many bloody tumbles. Dance partners had suffered through Tilly's painful missteps on their sore feet, and learned to slow dance with her.

When Tilly walked, she carefully looked down at her feet. This failed to prevent her from falling face down on hard cement thanks to cracks in the sidewalk. When Tilly had a major fall and sustained eight sprains in her left foot and two fractures in her ankle, her physical rehabilitation team evaluated her feet.

The left foot was noticeably larger than her right foot. After measurement, it was determined that Tilly's feet were two sizes apart. Tilly began to search for a custom shoe store that would sell her walking shoes in two different sizes for her odd-sized feet.

After one year, she found her shoes at a store for different-sized feet. The handsome store manager helped Tilly overcome her self-consciousness. He also had feet that were one-and-a-half sizes apart. At closing time, he asked Tilly to dinner and she accepted.

Two years later, Tilly and the shoe store manager married. Tilly had found her sole mate.

OUT OF TIME

The second hand on her wristwatch ticked in Sue Ann's head like an itch she needed to scratch. *Tick, tick, tick,* she heard it say as she counted her remaining time in measuring spoons. She owed Fast Frankie fifty thousand dollars for a gambling debt, which she knew she couldn't repay.

He was on his way over to her flophouse to collect and she knew she was done. She made coffee and prepared for the worst. Frankie burst through the door like he owned the place and flung himself on her dumpy sofa.

"Coffee?" Sue Ann asked.

"Can you add some creamer to it? My ulcers have been killing me," he said.

"Sure, Frankie," she answered.

Sue Ann brought the coffee to Frankie. He took a sip and got right to the point. "Do you have my money?" he asked.

"Yes, Frankie. I'll get it from the bedroom," Sue Ann answered.

After a few minutes, Sue Ann heard the coffee cup fall onto the ceramic floor and shatter. She ran into the living room where Fast Frankie was stone-dead with his eyes wide open.

"It must have been his bleeding ulcers," Sue Ann told Detective Patterson.

CONFESSION

"Bless me, Father, for I have sinned. It has been one year since my last confession," Irene O'Shaughnessy said.

"Continue," responded Father O'Reilly.

"I have been with so many men that I lost count."

"What do you mean by 'been with'?" asked the priest.

"Sex, Father, sex," Irene responded.

"Please lower your voice. The other parishioners who are waiting in line for confession can hear you," Father O'Reilly said. "Why do you have sex with these men? Are you in relationships with them?"

"No, Father. They were all one-night stands," Irene answered.

"How did you have so many one-night stands that you lost count?" the priest asked.

"Must be the booze. I walk to the pub around the corner from my flat every night for a bit of bubble and squeak, have a few pints, and the next thing I know, I'm done for," answered Irene.

"Don't you cook?" asked Father O'Reilly.

"No, Father. I never learned how," Irene said.

"For your penance, say the rosary, buy a cookbook, start making your own dinners, and stay away from The Irish Hound for one year," said Father O'Reilly. "Can you do that Irene?"

"I'll try Father," she agreed. "How did you know it was me?"

"See you next year, Irene. Merry Christmas to you," answered Father O'Reilly.

"Same as last year," he muttered under his breath.

"Next," he called.

MASQUERADE BALL

Miss Eddie's great-niece, Delilah Deveraux, had returned from a year abroad in Europe. Her aunt surprised Delilah with the news that the southern masquerade ball would be held in the Deveraux ballroom. At eighteen, Delilah stopped young men in their tracks with her striking beauty. Known for her long, raven black hair, clear blue eyes, and shapely figure, Delilah had already perfected the art of flirtation to her advantage.

Delilah, a vision in a flowing, black silk gown, large, red-feathered hat slanted down over her right eye, and gold-sequined mask, brought conversation to a halt as she descended the marble staircase into the ballroom. Her attire complemented the red velvet and gold-leaf furnishings of the Victorian-era room. Music, conversation, and excited suitors filled the room by the time Delilah stepped onto the ballroom floor.

Delilah threw back her head and laughed at compliments while she danced across the room with one partner after another. Suddenly, voodoo took hold of Delilah, who floated across the room toward a black-masked man. He had long dark hair, and wore a black hat and a black velvet cape.

"You must be my Delilah," he whispered softly to her in a European accent.

"My name is Sam," he said, and pulled her frame tightly against his strong build.

He continued to whisper in Delilah's ear. She was lost to this one man, and only this man, who wore a gold ring with the numbers 616 in Greek on it. "You shall be mine forever," he said, and whisked her out of the ballroom. Smoke followed once the Deveraux ballroom doors closed behind them.

"The devil you know is better than the devil you don't," the single females murmured among themselves.

ON THE RUN

He had a head start and took off in a panic. His heart raced as he ran faster and faster. His life depended on it. In the mountains of Virginia, his masters had sent the hounds out after him.

Though terrified, he ran up and down hills, to the right and left of woodlands to throw them off his scent. He leapt over ponds without taking a sip of water, which he needed badly. There was no time to think about hydration. *Just keep running*, he thought in dread.

Then he heard hooves racing in the distance. They were coming after him on horses. He ran faster, but heard the dogs' howling getting closer to him. He had to break away fast.

He crossed a stream, jumped into an open hole, and dug himself deeper in the ground. He heard the hounds and horses turn around and head in the other direction. He was free now to rest.

After three hours, the terror began to melt away. It was March and the ground was freezing, but he was safe. The hunt had ended for the red fox.

No one would be smeared with his blood today.

GRADY CRAWLEY

Grady Crawley hissed, cursed, grunted, and spat, but he never spoke to any neighbors. His greasy hair, oil-stained clothes, and jagged brown teeth were more than enough to chase the large black crows away. His neighbors were forced to endure this loathsome creature from dawn until dusk while he worked in his eyesore of a front yard. Grady had planted drought-resistant desert plants ten years earlier to avoid hefty water bills in Sierra Vista, Arizona.

The plants were overgrown, brown, and filled with spiked thistles. Grady did have one companion—a parrot named Horatio who was kept outside in a cage under cover on the front porch. While his human owner cursed at the city workers who parked their trucks in front of his termite-infested shack, Horatio mimicked every word his owner said. This only worsened an adversarial relationship between Grady and the town of Sierra Vista.

Local officials took offense at Grady's behavior and looked into every aspect of the property that he occupied: ownership, property taxes, code violations, and weed and mosquito abatement. Grady had full ownership of the dwelling and property granted in his divorce settlement from a local real estate broker who was only too happy to walk away from it—and Grady as well. His property taxes were paid twice each year by his ex-wife as part of the divorce settlement.

The dwelling needed a paint job, new roof, repaired driveway, and new fence, all of which violated the property's homeowners association's Covenants, Conditions, & Restrictions. A list of necessary work was sent to Grady's HOA, which mailed it to him, along with a due date for completion and applicable fines. The question of weed abatement was debatable because of the height and condition of his drought-resistant plants. A list of acceptable plants was also forwarded to Grady by his HOA, with a due date for replacement and applicable fines. Mosquito abatement violations did not apply, because he did not have a swimming pool or standing water on the property.

When the postal worker delivered the HOA notices to Grady, he ripped them open, sat down in the center of his yard, and cursed up a dust storm that lasted for three days. During this time, Horatio repeated the cursing, causing the neighbors to complain to city hall and the HOA. The verbiage and volume used by Grady had disrupted the neighborhood and scared off families with small children.

Finally, the local police drove over to have a talk with Grady about the commotion. Predictably, they were cursed up one side and down the other, first by Grady and then by Horatio. Grady's foul cursing of the police quickly escalated to fighting. He was cuffed and taken away on several charges, never to return.

Oddly enough, Horatio stopped cursing once the police drove away with Grady. The family next door adopted Horatio and kept him inside. Horatio learned to sing along both high and low to operetta.

BACKFIRED

"If I can't have him, no one else can," screamed the dark-haired, crystal blue-eyed art maven from the back of a dark alley.

A voluptuous, curly-haired blonde in skintight jeans and a teal tank top slowly backed away from the screaming woman holding a gun.

"Stop or you'll get it," she threatened.

The blonde continued to move backwards toward the front of the alley.

A tawny cat jumped from a roof overhead onto a garbage can, startling the woman with the gun. She pulled the trigger and the gun backfired, causing her to fall to the ground. She dropped the gun, held her hands over her right eye, and screamed, "My eye. My eye!"

The blonde ran to safety out into the street. "I've called an ambulance for you," she yelled. "You can have the painting if it means that much to you," she offered.

Who knew my painting would cause so much trouble, the blonde thought to herself. *An artist's life is fraught with pain and suffering,* she reflected, and disappeared into the night.

FIRST KISS

He scooped her up in his arms, and she wrapped her arms around his neck. He lowered his face to hers, stared at her rose-shaped lips, and gently touched them with his in a soft, warm kiss.

"That was my first kiss," she said.

"I know," he said, and smiled.

Then he kissed her again.

TROUBLE IN CHINATOWN

Ian "Sully" Sullivan, the house dick at the Lotus Flower flophouse in San Francisco's Chinatown, was in hot water. It was Sunday morning, and while he was supposed to be on duty the night before, the safe had been cleaned out. Sully had heard an earful from the owner and knew his job and room were on the line.

He worked the entire evening over in his mind while he drank some freshly-brewed black coffee. Damn if he hadn't been behind that crummy registration desk the whole evening, taking cash from drunks and couples who paid for rooms by the hour. All he'd done was entertain a blonde dish in his room for a couple of hours at 2:00 a.m. when the coast was clear. That was all, but it had been enough time for someone to clean out the safe of the rundown dump.

Mr. McFarland, the owner, had told him a grand was taken from the safe. Something didn't smell right to Sully. However, money was money and he had to get it back.

He waited until midnight and walked down the three steep blocks to China Lil's, where he'd first met the blonde doll. She wasn't there. He asked Lil if she'd seen her, and was told she hadn't been around for a couple of days. Sully threw down a quick glass of plum wine, pulled the fedora over his forehead, and walked back up the three steep blocks to the Lotus Flower.

No one was around, so he went to lay down on his bed for a few minutes. When he opened the door to his room, he was surprised to see the dame sitting in his chair, thumbing through a magazine. She must have liked what he'd served and wanted more.

She stood up, wrapped her arms around his neck, and started kissing him. "Hey, honey, not so fast," Sully said. "I don't know anything about you."

"What's there to know, sweetie?" she asked. "I like you. I like you a lot."

"Have you ever been in the can?" Sully pulled back, narrowing his eyes at her.

"Hey, why are you giving me the third degree?" She scrunched up her face in frustration and backed away from him.

"The safe was robbed while we were busy the other morning, that's why," he answered.

"My old man was in the hoosegow because he nicked the cash register at the diner where I work when I was outside on break. Listen, mister, I didn't have anything to do with that, or him, since it happened. I don't want any trouble," she said.

"Do you have a photograph of him you can loan me?" he asked.

She reached into her purse, pulled a small photo out of her wallet, and handed it to him.

"Where does he like to hang out, baby?" Sully asked.

"The back room of No Fu Lin's on Market and 8th. There's a card game going every night after 10:00 p.m.," she answered.

"Okay, honey. I want you to stay out of sight while I track him down and get the money back. Deal?" asked Sully.

"Deal," she said, and left with a sigh.

The next evening, Sully cleaned his gun and loaded it with bullets. He staked out No Fu Lin's and waited in the alley around the corner.

When he saw the doll's ex, he grabbed him around the neck and dragged him into the alley, the gun jabbed into his back.

"I want the grand you stole from me Sunday morning, plus a C-note for getting me in hock with my manager," Sully said.

"Don't get trigger happy, mister. I'll give you the dough," the ex said. He reached into his pocket, took out a wad of cash, and counted out ten one hundred dollar bills, plus one extra for Sully. Then he held the cash to the side and Sully took it.

"One more thing—leave the blonde doll alone. I'm seeing her now. Got it?" Sully asked.

"Got it," the ex said, and left.

Sully replaced the grand in the safe, which satisfied McFarland, who gave him Saturday night off.

The blonde dish was taken out for the first of many evenings of dinner and dancing with Sully in Frisco's Chinatown.

ORVILLE DUFFY

Orville Duffy had lived his entire life in Last Chance, Mississippi. He was thirty-five, six feet tall, and two hundred pounds of unremarkable human flesh and bone, except for one observation—Orville had a middle flicker finger on his right hand. The entire population of three hundred and twenty-five people had experienced the appearance of Orville's middle finger in their faces, children watching in awe. His middle finger had a long black fingernail, which hadn't been cleaned in years.

Orville's affliction of middle flicker finger syndrome unsettled the town's residents because he worked as a grave-digger at the only cemetery in Last Chance. During solemn graveside burials and funerals, Orville's middle finger flicked out in the most inopportune moments at close range. The words *good*, *holy*, *thoughts*, and *prayers* set off Orville's finger during eulogies.

Father Thomas, the town's only clergy, had experienced the worst of it during his eulogies. Father's eulogy opener, "He was a *good* and *holy* man," received two flicks of Orville's middle finger, as did, "Let us keep the dearly departed in our *thoughts* and *prayers*."

The people attending Mr. Heinz's recent burial were perplexed by Father Thomas's eulogy: "Bob Heinz lived high on the hog, not off the fat of the land. He knew his onions from his toil of the soil. He left his family with shelter from the storm. Make no bones about it, he is now over the moon. Be like Bob. That's the full Monty," he said, and walked away quickly.

The group dispersed, and Orville calmly buried the casket. Father Thomas spoke Orville's language, with which his middle finger agreed.

SHADOW MAN

One dark and foggy night in Seaside, Oregon, Tessa, a lifelong insomniac, awoke to the smell of smoke. As a cigarette smoker, she immediately recognized the smoke to be that of a cigarette. However, there were five other women in the tri-level home, they were renting for the summer, all of whom were fast asleep.

Tessa knew none of the other women smoked. She quietly slipped out of bed, positioned her back flat against the wall, and peeked through the doorway for a second. Imagine her terror when she saw a tall, thin, shadowy man sitting cross-legged on the fireplace hearth downstairs. He was chain-smoking cigarettes.

She immediately thought of a plan to scare the intruder off. Tessa quietly awakened her friend, Pat, who stood over six feet tall with short, dark hair. Tessa apprised her of the situation and asked her to stand in the doorway, her back toward the intruder, and trick him into thinking there was a man in the house.

Pat stood in the doorway for a few moments, her back toward the intruder, just as Tessa had suggested, then she quietly returned to the bedroom. When Tessa looked through the doorway again, the smoke was gone and so was the intruder.

Tessa and Pat slipped downstairs and noticed a window next to the fireplace had been opened from inside, the screen left ajar. They closed the window, checked the rest of the house, and found the front door locked. After determining that the shadowy smoker was long gone, they decided he must have had a key to the rental home.

The next morning, Tessa had the lock to the front door changed. The four other females slept soundly through the night, and never questioned why the lock had changed. Tessa had learned rentals offered an open invitation to unwelcome intruders of all kinds.

THE VIOLINIST

The incessant *rat-a-tat-tat* of rain beat down on the drenched fishing village in Nova Scotia until a haze of gloom hung over the dark, dreary hamlet. The small enclave was devoid of tourists—or any sign of life, for that matter. Even the lighthouse tube was out.

Suddenly, a violin echoed the beat of the rain. As the rain picked up, the violinist played faster and faster in time with the rain. When the rain poured down on the village, the violinist played in a state of frenzy.

In the darkness, the rain and music stopped. The hum of the lighthouse tube started up. Then the light illuminated an ocean of battered, broken, and unsalvageable fishing boats.

The music of the violinist was never heard again.

FINE DINING

Mort's relationship with Phoebe had become stale. No more movies, concerts, day trips, or fun, all of which they had experienced during the early weeks of dating. He made a decent income, but selfishly spent money on his own hobbies: photography, rock climbing, and scuba diving, none of which interested Phoebe.

Phoebe's precious Saturday nights had been reduced to Mort bringing over his weekly laundry for her to wash and dry. He even refused to buy laundry detergent. She began to dread Saturday nights with Mort.

Mort called early one Saturday. "I thought I'd pick up takeout before coming over. You have your choice of In-N-Out Burger, Taco Bell, or Jack in the Box," he said.

Phoebe, a health-conscious young female, replied, "Don't bother. I'm having a vegetarian salad before I go to a yoga retreat."

HUNTRESS

The dame paced back and forth in her spiked high heels, like a panther ready to pounce. Her tight black sweater and pants and short, dark hair suited the study of animal trophies on the walls and the leopard rug on the floor. Smoke belched out of her snub nose while she smoked a cigarette.

Velma Richards was used to getting what she wanted and, if she couldn't get it willingly, she found a way—dead or alive, like the animal heads mounted on the walls.

Velma had wanted Hank Anderson ever since her return to the family ranch she'd inherited in Virginia. She'd shown up after the estate was settled and she was named sole beneficiary. Hank ran the ranch and Velma wanted total control of him.

Velma didn't care about Hank's wife and three children who lived in a small ranch house on the grounds. She only cared about herself and had made a play for Hank's affection during the past three months. Her candlelit evening dinners in the mansion to discuss business; stolen kisses whenever she could put her hands all over him; he was hers and she would have him for keeps, one way or another.

Hank was expected at the main house by 9:00 p.m. and he was ten minutes late. By the time the doorbell rang, Velma had worked herself into a frenzy. She snuffed out her cigarette and stretched out leisurely on an animal skin couch. Hank was escorted into the study by a butler who poured drinks for two and left.

"Velma, you have the wrong idea about us," Hank said. "I'm not leaving my family. Don't get me wrong. It's been fun, but my wife needs me to help out with our children. I just learned we have another little one on the way."

"The hell with that!" screamed Velma, who pointed a pistol deadeye at Hank. "If I can't have you, no one can."

"No, Velma," Hank warned. "Don't do something you'll regret for the rest of your life."

"Regrets? I have never had a single regret," Velma yelled. Before she could pull the trigger, she dropped the pistol and fell back against the couch. Blood seeped out from her torso onto the couch.

The butler lowered his gun and went to her as she was dying. "If I can't have you, no one can, Velma," he said to her, and shut her eyes.

He turned back around to Hank. "I used to be her husband," Rollo, Velma's ex-husband said.

ROOM 76

The door of Room 76 at Our Lady of Sorrows Hospital in Bedford, New York had an annoying habit of opening on its own. The hospital administrator had considered tightening the door hinges, but her predecessor had done that to no avail. Therefore, the staff and patients lived with the door that seemed to open for no reason at all.

One All Hallows' Eve, the wind was blowing down trees and power lines all over the city. From outside the hospital, a faint glow could be seen coming from the inside of Room 76. An outline of twenty-two Puritans in late sixteenth century garb could barely be seen surrounding the bed.

A small, dark shadow in a hospital gown sat up, raised two hands high in the air as if to strangle someone, and the twenty-two Puritans fell to the floor. All had been strangled.

The door of Room 76 opened, the smell of putrid smoke leaving the room and filling the hallway.

An orderly opened the hospital double doors to eliminate the foul stench.

Inside Room 76, he heard a small child's voice repeating, "Atone and be saved or suffer the noose."

Yet, no earthly being was in the room when he looked, only a ruffled bed.

THE SECRET KEEPER

"Good afternoon. Schlicher, Flicher, and Klicher," answered the law firm receptionist. "May I help you?" she asked.

A middle-aged gentleman who waited at the tall reception counter could not see where the voice came from until he bent over the top.

"Well, I'll be," he said. "Aren't you a bit young to be working?"

A nine-year-old girl in a business suit looked up and smiled at him. She responded, "I am Mr. Schlicher's daughter, Ella. How can I help you today?"

"Oh, Ella, of course you are! My name is Tony Correa. Could you please let him know I'm here for our two o'clock appointment?" he asked.

"Of course, Mr. Correa. Please take a seat and I'll tell him."

Ella picked up the receiver and punched the button for her father's private line. "Mr. Correa is here to see you," she said.

She hung up the phone and looked up at Mr. Correa. "He is ready for you. Please go in," Ella said.

Ella returned to taking a message and finishing up her typing while listening to dictation.

At four feet tall with her hair pulled back in a ponytail, Ella was a force of nature. She drank coffee, commanded an efficient reception area, and was all business.

She saw the ups and downs of human frailty pass through the double doors of her father's law firm: one of her father's best friends, Manny Hawn, an electric shock treatment patient; a woman who had given birth to a baby with bacterial meningitis caused by foodborne bacteria from eating undercooked meat at a Mongolian buffet; an underage adolescent accused of assaulting a young female; an elderly woman whose only son was trying to take her country manor and put her in a nursing home; and the father of a son who had written a forged check and absconded with a quarter of his wealth.

Ella learned a lot about life while she kept her father's secrets.

Unbeknownst to his family, her father tried divorce cases, helped his friends who saw him pro bono, donated needed items to people of different religious and political backgrounds than his own, and believed a handshake to be one's bond.

Ella valued the ability to hold confidences and retained this skill—developed at an early age—for the rest of her life.

THE LONG WAVE GOODBYE

Ella's mother, Elena Schlicher, used to speak with her daughter outside in the backyard of their suburban ranch-style home while Ella smoked her long, thinly tapered cigarettes. Elena knew her daughter was unhappy living at home, but there was nothing she could change. Ella worked for her father, a country lawyer, during holidays and vacations. She also helped her mother with all the household chores. Ella had a hard time working for both of her parents, was sleep deprived, and suffered from chronic fatigue.

"So, you call your life here a 'prison,' and you cannot wait to leave," Elena said, inhaling the smoke from her daughter's cigarette.

"What do you think, Mom?" asked Ella. "Lockdown every night at 9:00 p.m. Off to work with Dad at 6:30 a.m. weekdays, and home by 7:30 p.m. Kitchen cleanup with you every night after dinner. On Saturdays, we return to the office for janitorial service. Then, rise and shine on Sunday for Mass, and help you change the sheets of four beds, wash the floors, and make dinner. I've never had time to myself. Until I leave here, I never will."

"Your father is not a wealthy man. We need to pitch in and help out around here. That's how it is," her mother answered.

"I'm sixteen now and feel like a hired hand. My sisters and all my friends have stay-overs, take music lessons, go to summer school, swim, and have normal lives. But no. I'm the only girl I know who works the same hours as her father," complained Ella.

"I'm sorry you feel this way, Ella," her mother replied. "You'll be going away to college soon. I've always done my best by you, and I always will."

"I know, Mom. I'm sorry to dump on you like this. You're the only one I can talk to in this place. I do appreciate that," Ella said.

"I'll miss our talks when you're gone," Elena answered, and slowly walked away.

Me too, Ella thought to herself.

Three months later, Ella looked through the back window of the twenty-year-old Oldsmobile, saw her mother in the kitchen window waving at her, and she waved back until her mother was long out of sight. Saying goodbye to her mother always left Ella feeling lost, with a lump in her throat and eyes welled up with tears. How Ella already missed and loved her.

She thought of her mother washing and drying the dishes, pots and pans, and silverware without her. She wouldn't be there to help her change the sheets and wash the floors every week. Her mother was going to have to do all the household chores alone. Then there was the grocery shopping, filling up the car with gas, gardening, and laundry; the list was endless.

She thought of her mother's tiny closet, and the Christmas gifts she saved for the family all year long; her mother's laundry line of clothes in the backyard; the ironing board in the laundry room where her mom stood and ironed the family's clothes, including the sheets.

Ella wished she could ask her father to turn the car around so she could give her mother the hug and kiss she deserved. She felt small and selfish, and would have given anything to take her words back. Ella missed her mother terribly and she was still in town.

Her amends would have to wait until next time when she returned and held her mother in her arms.

A HOMELESS MAN

A posted notice appeared in the schools, markets, and churches of Henderson, Nevada:

A homeless man has been sleeping in our neighborhood park off River Drive. He is in his 40's, and has a grocery cart with his stuff in it. I walked by the park this evening and saw this man asleep against a tree. I am worried about our children. Has anyone else seen him?

After one week, a notice on purple paper with colorful homemade paper flowers was posted on a tree near the park in response to the inquiry:

I am the wife of the homeless man. He has been a resident of Henderson for his entire life. We have been married twenty-five years and have three children and two grandchildren.

All the items in the cart belong to him except for the cart, which he found in the street. My husband is a veteran with post-traumatic stress disorder. He wants everyone to leave him alone and is working with the Veterans Administration to get him a place of his own soon. My children, grandchildren, and I love him more than words can say.

THE MAGIC OF MINICH ISLE

Every summer, Marcus Helmsfeld was thrilled when he and his family returned to Minich Isle, a small outer island off the northern coast of New Zealand. It was only on Minich Isle that Marcus truly felt a sense of belonging. His great-grandfather had built the Helmsfeld stone and mortar home, which sat on a hill of soft green grass overlooking the sea. There was a stone outbuilding on the property where the surfboards, bicycles, and motorbikes were safely stored.

An old swing hung from the puriri tree with his boyhood fort at the top near the front of the Helmsfeld home. Although Marcus's wife had passed three years earlier from cancer, he brought his two twin six-year-old sons, Phil and Pato, and his fifteen-year-old daughter, Malinda, with him to Minich Isle every summer from November until early February. He wanted his children to enjoy the wonder of the outdoors the way he had as a youngster. Back in the urban life of Sydney, Australia, Marcus and his children were deprived of outdoor living and exploration. He worked as a pediatrician and was often called away for emergencies. Marcus longed to spend more time with his children.

Pulling up to the Helmsfeld retreat, the air was cooler and easier to breathe, the sky was bluer, and the greens of summer showed off in a palette of brilliant colors. Marcus and his children brought their luggage and groceries inside and settled in quickly. While the boys ran outside and played in the fort, his daughter, Malinda, rocked contentedly back and forth in the swing.

Marcus stood outside on the top floor balcony and inhaled the cool, fresh air. He smiled at the sight of his children frolicking. Then he turned his attention to the calm, bluish-green ocean below. Marcus vowed he would rise before the children and surf alone the next morning.

Walking to the beach in the quiet tranquility of the early hours in the morning, Marcus met his friend, Tim, who was also bound for surfing. The two friends hugged and paddled out on their surfboards together in the morning mist. A wave came up and Marcus took it easily, surfing along a straight line. He felt better than he had in years.

Marcus and Tim surfed many waves almost effortlessly. Out near where the sun was rising, Tim pointed out dolphins jumping in and out of the water, one after another. Back on the sand, Marcus dried himself off, waved goodbye to Tim, and carried his surfboard back to the stone outbuilding.

Inside the home, the smell of homemade cinnamon buns, coffee, bacon, and eggs warmed his heart and stomach.

His daughter, Malinda, was growing up fast, and had made breakfast for the family. The boys were already nibbling on their second cinnamon buns.

"Well, what shall we do with our day?" Marcus asked his crew.

"I need to go into town for personal items," said Malinda.

"We want ice cream," squealed the twins in delight.

"The town it is," laughed Marcus. "We'll leave once this kitchen is cleaned up."

An hour later, Marcus pulled up near a lush, green park surrounded by a few shops in Minich. Malinda headed off to the pharmacy and agreed to meet her father and the boys in the park in an hour. Marcus took Phil and Pato to the Minich Confectionary. Inside, the boys stared in amazement at homemade fudge, taffy, chocolate brownies, and penny candies behind the glass display cases. In back of the confectionary, Marcus smiled, seated on a stool at the soda fountain.

"What shall it be, boys?" he asked.

"Double chocolate fudge sundae," they answered together.

A good-natured elderly woman walked out from behind two swinging doors. "Why, look who's returned for the summer. Welcome back, Helmsfelds! I heard your order from the back," greeted Betsy, the owner. "What will you have, Marcus?" she asked.

"A root beer float, if you don't mind, Betsy," Marcus answered.

While Betsy started to prepare Marcus's drink, a young female brought the double fudge sundae to the boys. It was piled high with hot chocolate fudge sauce, whipped cream, nuts, three scoops of vanilla ice cream, and two cherries on top. The boys giggled in delight, started eating, and were quiet.

"How have you been, Betsy?" Marcus asked, sipping his drink.

"Oh, I've been busier than ever. The summer festival is next Saturday at the park, and we're going to have an ice cream booth there. Everyone in town will be at the festival," Betsy said.

"We always enjoy the fireworks at night. It looks like we'll be going again this summer," Marcus said.

"There's a box lunch raffle this year," Betsy volunteered. "The donations will go to repair the school."

"It sounds like fun," Marcus responded thoughtfully.

Marcus laughed when he saw the sundae had been quickly devoured by Phil and Pato. "Come on, boys. Let's throw the ball around at the park," Marcus said. "Thanks for the sweets, Betsy. We'll see you next Saturday."

Marcus held the door open for Phil and Pato who collided with Jasmine Martin, his deceased wife, Seraphina's best friend. The papers she carried had scattered down the sidewalk. Phil and Pato chased the papers carried by the wind and tried to pick them up. "Marcus Helmsfeld!" Jasmine exclaimed, and gave him a hug.

"I can see you're working hard at the school during summer vacation," Marcus said.

"I'm the principal now and have admissions to review for the new school year," responded Jasmine. "Is Malinda with you as well?" she asked. Malinda hurried from the pharmacy, ran to Jasmine and gave her a big hug. "I've missed you so much, Jasmine. We need to have a long talk," Malinda said.

"I've missed all of you too," said Jasmine. "Are you going to the summer festival next Saturday?" she asked.

"Of course we are," said Malinda excitedly.

The boys brought the papers to Jasmine, who stuffed them in her shoulder briefcase. "I'll look forward to seeing all of you then. I'm making a box lunch for auction," she said, and smiled.

The Helmsfelds waved goodbye to Jasmine. Then they walked across the street to the park where Marcus and the boys threw a softball back and forth. Malinda walked across the park to a wooden bench and paused. Looking down, she saw the writing, *Marcus loves Seraphina,* carved inside of a heart in the hardwood. Malinda carefully sat down on the bench and gazed out upon the calming waters of the ocean. She thought about her mother and how much she loved her, and her best friend, Jasmine.

Driving home, Marcus reflected on Seraphina, who had grown up on Minich Isle in a cottage next to the school. He'd met her at the age of ten while on summer vacation. They'd immediately became good friends, fallen in love as adolescents, then married after Marcus had completed his residency. She had Malinda soon after they'd married, and the twins ten years later. Marcus was a pediatrician and had helped his wife deliver all their children.

His thoughts came back to Jasmine and the present. Her violet eyes and smile stirred something in him that he hadn't felt for a long time. He looked forward to seeing her at the summer festival next Saturday.

During the week, the Helmsfelds developed an easygoing rhythm that suited all. In the early mornings, Marcus enjoyed the sunrise, surfing, and dolphin watching with Tim. Malinda cooked breakfast, fed the twins, and cleaned up afterward. The rest of their days were spent riding bicycles, playing softball, collecting seashells on the beach, and wading in the cool, refreshing ocean water. At night, Dad barbecued shrimp, cod, and even lobster. After dinner, they sat around the fire pit and told ghost stories. Marcus would start the story, and each child added on to it. At night, they went to bed exhausted and slept well.

The Saturday of the Minich Summer Festival finally arrived. After cleaning up the kitchen, the Helmsfelds set off for the park. The usually quiet village was alive with colorful banners, balloons, and a myriad of games and vendors. Malinda wandered through the displays of handmade purses, velvety scarves, and sun hats. Suddenly, she saw a familiar face smiling at her.

"I've been wondering when I'd see my favorite girl," he said.

Malinda jumped up and gave him a big hug. "Jonathan, I've been wondering when I would see you too."

"Want to hang out together?" he asked.

"Of course," she said happily, and wandered off with Jon, hand in hand.

Marcus took the twins to the game booths. He watched his sons in amusement as they threw darts at balloons, rings around bottles, and coins into a dish. Phil and Pato didn't succeed in their attempts, but they had fun anyway.

Betsy stood at a microphone and made an announcement. "Good afternoon, everyone. The box lunch raffle will begin shortly. Please move to the seating area by the bandstand and take a seat if you plan to participate."

Marcus and the twins walked to the chairs and sat down. In a few minutes, the area was full. Betsy appeared on the stage again and said, "We have many lovely box lunches today. Today's proceeds will benefit improvements for our school. When you see a box lunch you'd like to bid on, please raise your hand and make an offer. The person with the highest bid will win a box lunch with the person who made it."

One female after another walked up to the microphone, described the scrumptious contents in their lunch baskets for two, and walked down to the person who bought them. The last female to bring up two large picnic baskets was Jasmine.

"I have a delicious lunch for five people," Jasmine announced. The crowd laughed in good humor at the amount of food Jasmine made.

Marcus raised his hand high in the air. "Fifty dollars for the lot," he said with a smile. The twins jumped up and down in their seats for having won at last. Jasmine walked down to Marcus, who took one lunch basket from her and followed her with the twins.

Jasmine spread a large, summery blanket on the grassy hill, which overlooked the ocean. She delicately arranged a spread of various meat sandwiches, potato salad, cheese, crackers and a chocolate cake in front of the boys. Marcus placed the plates, utensils, napkins, and juice bottles on the blanket.

Marcus handed her the plates, one at a time while she filled each with sandwiches and salad. After the boys had started on their lunches, Jasmine and Marcus filled their plates and sat down to eat. Marcus and Jasmine looked out at the sun shining on the water below like diamonds. They sat close together and quietly savored the food and view as if they had done this every Saturday at the park.

The twins helped themselves to cheese, crackers, and more juice. Before long, they were fast asleep. The group of Helmsfelds looked like a young, loving family that was content in their solitude. Jasmine rested her head on Marcus's shoulder and she also dozed off. While she slept, Marcus held her hand.

When the twins awoke, it was dark. Malinda and Jon had joined the group and finished the sandwiches. Soon enough, music drifted in from the bandstand on the other side of the park. Malinda and Jon hurried off to dance.

Jasmine and Marcus were awakened by the music and surprised to find that Phil and Pato had removed the cake cover. "Time for cake, boys?" Jasmine asked. The boys squealed in delight as Jasmine served each of them a large, gooey piece of chocolate fudge cake.

Marcus fully enjoyed the cake too. It had been a long time since he and his children had enjoyed a picnic together while he rested. All he could think of was that he wanted more of their afternoon together, more Saturdays, and most of all, more of Jasmine.

Excitement rang through the Minich Summer Festival as word that the fireworks were about to start filtered through the crowd. Malinda and Jon came and took the boys to a lookout for a good view of the show. Marcus told Jasmine, "I want to take you somewhere with me."

Marcus led Jasmine by the hand to the wooden bench where he had first kissed Seraphina thirty years ago. While the fireworks were set off from boats out in the ocean, Marcus and Jasmine enjoyed the colorful display of fireworks in the sky, reflected in the water below. The winds had turned offshore and were blowing the smoke from the boats out to sea.

Caught up in the romance of stargazing, he gazed lovingly at Jasmine and kissed her deeply. He looked over her shoulder and saw a star that fell, made a right-angle turn, sped off, and disappeared. In that magical split second, Marcus realized he had come home.

SLICK

Lorelei's large, flouncy blouses, which presented her big breasts to their best advantage, and talkative nature were her ticket to male companionship wherever she went. She wasn't the type of woman that men would take out more than once, but she was easy to be with. Lorelei kept her barstool warm at the Giddyap Bar in Midland, Texas nearly every night of the week.

It was a slow Tuesday night and Lorelei was chatting up the bartender, Billy Buck. Then a long-legged, weather-worn cowboy in jeans, boots, and a ten-gallon hat sauntered in and took a seat at the bar next to Lorelei. "How do, missy? Can I buy you something to warm you up?" the cowboy asked, leaning into Lorelei.

"Scotch neat would be mighty nice," she said, flipping her light brown hair behind her shoulders.

"Make that a double for me," he said, and grinned at Billy.

"What's your name, stranger?" Lorelei asked.

"Jimmy Jay Jackson," he said.

"Mine is Lorelei and I work as an office manager at Dawton Oil," she said.

"It's a small world, honey. I worked on an oil rig for Dawton before I was laid off last year," he responded.

Billy slid their drinks down the slick, lacquered counter to them.

"What are you doing now?" Lorelei asked as she reached into her open shoulder bag to pull out a pack of cigarettes.

Jimmy Jay pulled himself closer to Lorelei while he lit her cigarette.

"I'm looking for work," he answered.

"Dawton is hiring again if you want to give us another shot," she suggested.

Jimmy Jay downed his drink, stood up, put a twenty-dollar bill on the counter, and said abruptly, "I best be moving on. I have a lead on a job waiting for me in Laredo."

Lorelei's jaw fell as she watched Jimmy Jay rush out the door.

"Well, I'll be. Wonder if it was something I said. I better pay up and head on home," Lorelei said to Billy.

"No need to pay tonight," Billy answered, feeling sorry for her. She'd struck out and he couldn't work out why in his head, either.

"You're a true gentleman," Lorelei told Billy. "I'll see you tomorrow night," she said, and walked out the door.

Later that evening, Lorelei returned home and reached inside her shoulder bag for her wallet to put a few bills in the can for emergencies. When she dumped all the contents out on the kitchen table, she was shocked to find the wallet was missing.

While Jimmy Jay was lighting her cigarette, he had reached inside her open bag, grabbed the wallet in his large hand, and slipped it in his back pocket, slick as an oil spill.

THE PSYCHIC

Louisa, a forty-something information technology analyst, had an addiction she kept to herself—Gina, her psychic. Louisa had revealed a dark secret from her past to Gina six months ago, and the psychic had controlled her ever since. Whenever Gina called, Louisa hurried to her for a new revelation. Each visit cost Louisa seventy-five dollars, which she couldn't afford to spend.

Louisa's interest in the beyond had started at a young age when she'd found her astrology chart giftwrapped under the Christmas tree. Numerology, tarot card readings, handwriting analysis, and sessions with well-known psychics and mind readers were all part of her life. In fact, some of her best friends were psychics, but they couldn't help her undo the dark incident.

Louisa needed Gina's help to erase the stain from her past. One Saturday afternoon, Louisa rushed into Gina's office. There, Gina sat in a comfortable chair, rocking her baby back and forth in her arms. She told Louisa that the answer had finally been given to her.

"This is what you must do. Buy thirteen candles, then bring twelve women with you to a graveyard on the thirteenth of the month at 11:45 p.m. Light each candle, undress, and, at the stroke of midnight, dance in a circle around the candles thirteen times. Of course, if you cannot do this, I will take care of it for thirteen hundred dollars," Gina told her. She nodded knowingly, opening the bag hanging from her shoulder.

"Of course, I can do this. All of it. Thank you for solving my problem," said Louisa with a smile.

Lighter than she'd felt for months, Louisa walked out the front door.

Gina stopped rocking her baby and looked perplexed.

She had no idea her client belonged to a coven of witches.

BOOKENDS

"Where's my cell phone?" Mr. Atherton asked his spouse, Althea.

"I don't know, but I can hear it ringing," she answered, sipping her morning coffee.

"Would you please call my phone for me so I can find it?" Alfred asked.

"Oh! Wait a minute. I'm sitting on my phone and need to move the pillows on the couch to get to it," she answered.

"What's taking so long, Althea?" Alfred asked from down the hall.

"It's ringing. Can you hear your phone?" Althea asked.

"Turn down the speaker on your phone so I can hear mine," responded Alfred.

"It clicked off. Calling again," Althea said, her phone tightly clutched in her hand. "Did you check beside the bed?" she asked.

"Yes," Alfred answered.

"Is it in the office?" she asked.

"Not there," he answered.

"Are you charging it in the kitchen?" she asked, trying to be helpful.

"Nope," he answered.

"I'm calling again. Try checking the bathroom," Althea suggested.

"Found it," Alfred said.

Alfred returned to the living room where Althea looked confounded.

"I can't find my glasses. Have you seen them?" she asked her husband.

"I'm looking right at them. They're on top of your head," Alfred answered. He settled down on the couch, phone in hand. "Darn. Now I can't remember who I needed to call," he complained.

THE BLACK OF NIGHT

Bring on the night. Show me darkness as black as coal without a star in the sky. Clear, cold black night is my time. This is when I do my best work.

I soar in the black of night, high above the mountain peaks. Don't hold back the darkness. It shields me against harm.

There is only one thing I like better than the black of night. It's the taste of blood; red, nourishing blood. It bonds for eternity and grants immortality for us, only us.

Leave a window open.

MRS. ROSEWOOD'S WISHES

"Helena, come up here now," shouted her mother, banging her cane on the floor repeatedly from the top floor bedroom suite. "When I call you the first time, you are to get your fanny up here immediately. Do you hear me?" she yelled. "It's seven in the morning. I am waiting for my paper and breakfast," she screamed from her bed.

Helena, the youngest daughter in the Rosewood dynasty, had been bred to wait on her mother's every wish, especially during Mrs. R.'s senior years. Antithetical to the name Rosewood, at the age of forty, Helena's life as Hortense's daughter had been anything but rosy. Helena wore her grey hair in a bun, was morbidly obese, and had a bad back and fallen arches from constantly huffing and puffing up and down the three-floor hardwood staircase to serve her mother.

Helena knocked on Mrs. R.'s door and brought the heavy breakfast tray and morning newspaper to her.

"Finally," Hortense said. "Fluff up my pillows, daughter, and read the paper to me."

Helena helped her mother settle in, sat in a chair by the bed, and read the paper to her.

That morning, the bags under Helena's eyes were darker than usual. She had been up until the early hours of the morning, washing and drying the dishes, silverware, and pots and pans. Her mother was a penny-pincher, and had hired only one male servant to drive, garden, make household repairs, and perform all the tasks that her daughter could not.

Hortense did not skimp on her own food—she had a predilection for pâté de foie gras, quail, and Dom Pérignon champagne. Helena's diet consisted of fast food—mostly cheap burgers, fries, and shakes—which Neville, the male employee brought in for her.

Mrs. R. gave Helena her dinner order and sent her away with the tray and tasks for the day. Helena spent the day preparing her mother's quail dinner, cleaning the mansion, and changing her clothes. Promptly at 5:30 p.m., Hortense pounded the hardwood floor with her cane and demanded Helena's appearance with her dinner.

Helena, short of breath, knocked on Mrs. R.'s door, walked through with the heavy dinner tray, and settled it onto Hortense's lap. There on her plate was a large quail stuffed with mushrooms, a side of green beans, a Caesar salad, and a crystal glass of champagne. She waved her daughter away and licked her lips while she devoured her dinner.

Neville told Helena that she looked exhausted and should go to bed early. Helena did exactly that and asked him to take her mother's tray away when called. She had a long warm bath and slept well for the first time in months.

During the night, Hortense passed in her sleep. Dr. Finney noted that her mother's ongoing diet of quail as a delicacy had presented a problem. Quails scavenged for seeds, grains, and various insects, and during migration, they flew across the country adding other varieties of food to their diet—including hemlock.

NIGHTMARE

Maxim tossed and turned, ruminating over his missing fiancée in his sleep. His nightmare painted a disturbing story of a wet cobblestone walkway, a shipyard, rope, an axe, and his missing fiancée, adding new elements while he slept. Every night.

It was a cold winter, but Max awakened in the afternoons with a feverish sweat and drenched sheets. The whiskey from his flask helped steady his shaky hands while he dressed himself to go to work. He saw the signs of his missing fiancée posted in shop windows on his daily walk to his job.

Once Max walked through the doors of the Iron Siren, he hung up his coat, put on an apron, stood six feet tall behind the bar, and pounded his meaty fists on the counter. He tended the bar and broke up fights in this seedy establishment, frequented by sailors, and women who made a living from the touch of a man's hands. His fiancée, Daphne, had been one of these women when Max met her.

She'd moved in with Max, stayed home, and had a hot meal ready for him when he returned from work at midnight each night. Daphne had cleaned their apartment, washed and ironed clothes, and made a home for Max. He had believed her soft, low whispers of love, yearning, and desire to be his wife, and bear children.

After two years of domestic happiness, he'd believed she was the woman she showed herself to be, and asked her to marry him. Max had fallen in love—mind, body, and soul—with a woman who had proved herself worthy of his devotion. In return, he declared his undying love, asked for her hand in marriage, and put a diamond and gold band on her ring finger.

Occasionally, a sailor would question Max regarding the whereabouts of Daphne. However, once Daphne moved in with Max, she had never returned to the bar. This made her disappearance—and his subsequent nightmare—even more unbearable for him.

Fearful of the nightmare, Max drank himself into oblivion and passed out on the bed. Several heavy burlap bags hidden in a dark room of the nightmare were new additions. The word *Guilty* was written in red on each bag.

Max pushed himself off the bed, sweat dripping from his face. He walked slowly, as if in a trance, to the closet and opened it. Then, he pulled out a navy blue trunk hidden in the darkness.

His heart sank when he opened the trunk and saw several heavy burlap bags, which contained Daphne's dismembered remains.

THE BOTOX GANG

When Natalia Robertson turned forty, her best friend, Bab Babbit threw a champagne and Botox party for her. This remarkable occasion drew twenty-five of Natalia's female friends, including their friendly neighborhood dermatologist, who also lived in the well-heeled gated community of thirty homes in Charleston, South Carolina. At twelve noon, the women munched on cucumber finger sandwiches, sipped champagne, and eagerly waited for the main event.

Dr. Priscilla Prickerton placed a large medical bag on the coffee table in the living room and called the ladies in from the kitchen. After everyone was seated, Priscilla scanned the room. "Bab, you've been through this many times. Would you like to be first?" Priscilla asked.

"Delighted," Bab responded. She stood up and sat down on a red silk chair in the center of the group. Priscilla placed a pillow underneath Bab's head, handed a mirror to her and asked, "Where would you like a touch-up?"

"I have a frown line near the right side of my lip," Bab said.

"Raise your chin up, dear, and please don't move," Priscilla said.

When Bab was situated, Priscilla said, "You may feel a mosquito-like sting," and injected the Botox into Bab's frown line. She closed her eyes and winced when the needle made a crunching sound and pierced her skin. Priscilla quickly handed her some tissues, and said, "Now hold these on the spot for five minutes and keep your head in an erect position for two hours." A thin line of blood dripped from Bab's chin onto the red silk chair.

Dr. Prickerton spent the next four hours Botoxing each woman with one free treatment wherever requested. In light of her birthday, Natalia had two injections for two frown lines between her eyebrows. The doctor left with appointments for most of the women including one new customer, Natalia.

After one year of paying for Botox treatments from Dr. Prickerton, Natalia declined the offer of another Botox birthday party from Bab.

Instead, she gave herself the present of Botoxing her bladder muscle. No one had warned her that Botox injections may have the embarrassing side effect of urinary incontinence.

PINNING HER EARS BACK

Wetherly's nightly ritual of meticulously examining her features and skin in a magnifying, lighted mirror halted with a horrific discovery. Her ears stuck out from the side of her head due to years of pulling her thick, long hair tightly behind them. After a serious discussion with her mother, it was decided that Wetherly needed to have her ears pinned back by the family plastic surgeon.

She whined about the pain she had already endured to be beautiful, but her mother's mind was laser-focused on finding Wetherly a suitable husband. The financial burden of maintaining Wetherly in the style to which she had become accustomed weighed heavy on her family's bank account. While her mother clipped coupons and negotiated the cost of lamb chops with the local butcher, Wetherly's clothes were stored in the only guest room.

Wetherly was literally pushing her parents out of their own home. Her mother knew she had to act fast or her husband would. The date of Wetherly's appointment came, and her mother helped Wetherly settle into her hospital room, where she would remain for five days after surgery. Wetherly was already complaining about the absence of mirrors in the room. Mother kissed her daughter goodbye and reassured her that all would go well.

Privately, her mother was looking forward to peace and quiet alone with her husband. She enjoyed romantic dinners, walks, and watching television with her husband without their daughter underfoot. Her spouse wished that he and his wife could make their home a happy abode for two permanently.

Unfortunately, Dad's happiness was not to be. Back home, magnifying, lighted mirror in hand, Wetherly's piercing shriek shook the rafters. She had spent so many years studying her face, her large right eyebrow was permanently raised.

SOILED

"Isn't it too early for a second shot of whiskey?" asked Joe, the owner of the Pickled and Tickled Bar in Western Kentucky.

Ray Taylor, the thirtyish man who'd ordered another shot, looked like he hadn't slept in days. His wool jacket was as wrinkled as his weathered face. It was 9:00 in the morning and Ray wanted to drown his problems in whiskey.

"Mister, I'll have a pickled egg to go with that shot," Ray said.

Early on that cold Sunday morning, Ray and Joe were the only two people in the dive bar around the corner from an alley where homeless people were still asleep.

"Okay, I'll fix you up," answered Joe. "Looks like you have a lot on your mind."

"I'm headed to my uncle's funeral at noon. You know the Undergood Farm off the highway? Fred Undergood was my uncle," said Ray.

"Fred was a regular pool player here on Fridays, yes sirree. I heard he died of cancer," responded Joe. "You're not from around these parts, are you?"

"No, I'm from New Jersey," Ray answered. "I worked for a soil engineering company for corn."

"You don't say," Joe said.

"The soil was engineered to produce double bushels of corn per acre, but the soil is bad, really bad," Ray whispered under his breath, poking his fork at the pickled egg. "Folks working the soil and eating the corn have been dying of cancer. Now my uncle is dead from bad soil," Ray ruminated. Then he threw down his second shot of whiskey.

"What are they doing for the families?" asked Joe.

"Nothing. All they care about is making money. Loads of it," Ray answered. "I blew the whistle on them by calling the newspapers with the number of customers who have died from the toxic corn grown in bad soil, but I don't know the chemicals in it that caused their deaths. I stopped selling it six months ago. The corn was used to make ethanol to fill up vehicles for less money than gasoline. As soon as people became used to it, the price per gallon increased and now it costs even more than gas," Ray continued. "After my uncle's funeral, I'm going to Canada to work in salmon farming, but I have to stop on the way," Ray finished.

Ray settled up his bill with Joe and shuffled out of the bar with his head hung low.

One week later, Joe studied an article in the *West Kentucky Star News:* "New Jersey Soil Engineering Corporation Blown Up: No One Hurt, Thousands of Jobs Lost, and Out of Business."

BOURBON STREET NOCTURNE

Nick Harrington caught the scent of pungent gardenias as he drove his Oldsmobile convertible up the winding entrance to the Balmore Estate in New Orleans, Louisiana. He was a thirty-five-year-old private detective drowning in bills and needed a fast break before going under. He took in the old-moneyed Colonial estate before ringing the doorbell.

"Good afternoon, Mr. Harrington," the maid said once she had opened the massive door. "Mrs. Balmore is waiting for you in the parlor. Please follow me."

Nick got an eyeful of the Balmore lineage, hung in oil paintings for posterity, along the walls of the entryway. Inside the overly-furnished parlor, he inhaled the sumptuous Mrs. Renatta Balmore—all five foot, ten inches of pure beauty. Renatta was decked out in white from her high heels to the pearls around her neck.

"Thank you for coming, Mr. Harrington, on short notice," Renatta greeted him, extending a hand.

"You can call me Nick, honey," he responded, and looked her up and down.

"I'm Renatta," she responded. "Would you like a drink?"

"Not during business," he answered. "What can I do for you?"

She led him to an overstuffed white silk sofa where they both sat down.

"I like a man who gets to the point where business is concerned. I need you to get some film returned to me and you'll be well paid for your trouble," Renatta volunteered, stretching out her long legs on the plush white carpet.

"I assume you don't want your husband to know, baby," Nick volunteered.

"That's right, Nick. You're a fast learner. I like that in a man," Renatta said, looking him straight in the eye.

"Do you know who's blackmailing you?" Nick asked.

"No, but I have a letter," she answered, and handed him an envelope.

Nick took the letter from the envelope and read it while Renatta studied him like a last will and testament. "Are you going to help me?" she asked.

"I'll help you, baby, but you're going to have to be honest with me," Nick responded. "Let's go for a drive."

"I'll get my scarf," she said.

Nick drove Renatta off the premises and up Bourbon Street, listening to sultry jazz wafting out from the clubs. Then he pulled the coupe over to the side of the road, looked at her face, and read it like a book. "What is it you don't want your husband to know, honey?" he asked. "I want to know what kind of a jam you're dragging me into."

"My husband doesn't know I have a three-year-old baby girl. A girlfriend is taking care of her for me in Metairie. I sneak off every month, visit my baby, and pay my friend in cash. Someone must have seen me there and taken photos of us. I can't afford for my husband to find out," Renatta said.

"Who's the father?" Nick asked, intrigued.

"A soldier who died in the war. I married him before he left, and became pregnant three months later," she answered. "My husband doesn't know I was married before."

"What would happen if he found out?" Nick asked.

"He'd divorce me quicker than a hot cricket, and I'd be left with nothing," she said. "The Balmores like their women to be lily-white when they marry them, and Catholic."

The table was set, and Nick was ready to eat. "I like the scenery just the way it is, honey," he said. "I'll get the film back for you. It will cost ten bucks a day plus expenses."

Renata opened her purse and handed Nick a C-note. "This should keep you busy for a while," she said.

"It will. This is a handful, but you should reconsider dumping your husband. I smell a rat in the works," Nick answered. He drove Renatta back to the estate and left her off.

"I'll be in touch," she said. "I don't want him to find out."

It was dark by the time Nick returned to his dumpy room in a fleabag boarding house on Bourbon Street. The dame was on his mind the entire drive home. He knew she was holding back, but he didn't care. She was the shiny, pretty package he had been waiting for his entire life and he wanted her.

The next day, he drove to Metairie. He rested against a bench in the park on a hunch that her friend would show up with the three-year-old girl. Nick was about to give up when a young woman who resembled Renatta showed up with the girl. He did a double take when he saw the woman's features and wondered what type of twisted spider's web he was tangled in.

He walked back to his coupe, followed them to the house in Metairie, and parked across the street to stake it out. He put the top up on his car and settled in for the night. No one arrived or left the place all night.

Then, in the morning, he saw a large man with a hat covering his face open the door and let himself in. Nick sat up with a start and pulled out his camera. He started taking pictures when the guy left the house. The man looked familiar, but he didn't register.

Nick returned to his dump and developed the film in his darkroom, the closet. He hung the photographs up to dry and looked at them with astonishment. He locked his room, jumped in the coupe, and hightailed it to the library.

He sat at the microfilm machine, quickly turning the handle, and raced through newspaper articles. He found the million dollar photograph, printed it out, and returned to his room. Nick compared the photocopy to the photographs he had taken and had no doubt—Renatta's husband had visited the young woman and girl. *What game was she playing?* he wondered.

Nick was pacing back and forth on the worn carpet when he heard a knock on his door. He looked through the peephole and saw Renatta, not a moment too soon. He let her in and said she had some explaining to do.

"What are you talking about, Nick?" Renatta asked, sprawled out on the sofa.

Nick showed her the photographs and asked, "What kind of chump do you take me for? Your husband saw your 'friend' and 'daughter' yesterday. Who is this woman?" he asked, and flung the photo into her lap.

Renatta took a quick look at the photo and slumped back in the sofa. "She's my sister," said Renatta, choking up.

"Who's the girl?" asked Nick.

"My niece," she answered.

"Who's the father?" asked Nick.

"My husband," she responded.

"Why didn't you tell me the truth from the beginning?" Nick asked.

"I wanted the photographs so I could divorce him. He'll give me a sweet settlement to avoid the scandal and press. His family would disown him if word of this ever got out," Renatta confessed.

Nick collected the rest of the photographs and threw them at Renatta, then he slapped her hard across the face, and she slapped him back.

"You're a liar and a dirty blackmailer," he yelled at her.

"No, Nicky. I had plans for us, honey," she insisted.

"You're a black-hearted snake and can slither down someone else's storm drain," he said. "Get out of here and never bother me again," he ordered, and pushed her out of his room.

Nick laid down on the lumpy sofa and snickered. There was a wad of cash for him on the table next to it.

Must be old money, he thought.

THE GOLDEN HOUR

He walked up the dirt path to the beach cottage and all he could see was her beauty basking in the sunlight. She wore a straw hat with a large sunflower on it, which couldn't confine her gorgeous, long, white hair blowing in the summer breeze. A caregiver brought her tea and sandwiches and sat next to her reading a book.

The caregiver, Miss Ginny, stood up when she saw him approach. "Mr. Isles, we were expecting you to visit Ms. Sophie today. We have some iced tea and sandwiches laid out special for you. I'll be back in a little while," Ginny said. "Why don't you have a seat and visit with Ms. Sophie?"

"Good afternoon, Ms. Sophie. You look well," Mr. Isles said, picking up the book and sitting down.

"I know you've been here before, but I don't remember your name. I have a memory problem," Sophie said.

"Ferrell. My name is Ferrell Isles," he said.

"It's nice of you to think of visiting me, Mr. Isles. Please have some tea and sandwiches," Sophie answered.

"Thank you, Ms. Sophie." He helped himself to cucumber and salmon sandwiches and tea.

He gazed at the sun dancing on the ocean and asked, "Looks like diamonds on the water, don't you think, Ms. Sophie?"

"It sure does. I can't think of a more beautiful spot on the face of the earth. I love to sit here through the golden hour and soak it up. Would you care to read to me, Mr. Isles?" Sophie asked.

"I would love to read to you, Ms. Sophie," he answered.

"Let's see. What do we have here?" he asked. "*The Green of Summer* by William Ferrell Isles. That's an interesting title for a book."

"I love summer," she said. "The sky is bluer. I can smell the spray of salt water from the ocean in the air. Most of all, there are so many shades of green in the trees, shrubs, and even the grass that I would never be able to count them all," Sophie remarked laughing.

Mr. Isles laughed along with her. Then he opened the book, removed the bookmark, and started to read. He had a soothing reading voice that Ms. Sophie found most enjoyable. She smiled while listening, and watching the sun glisten on the water, eventually turning it to gold.

"Mr. Isles, why don't you stop for now. Let's watch the sunset together. This is my favorite time of day," she said.

"I'd enjoy that, Ms. Sophie," answered Mr. Isles.

Miss Ginny watched from the porch as Sophie and Ferrell sat together, enjoying the magnificent display of red, purple, and gold as the sun met the horizon and set over the sea.

Ms. Sophie extended her right hand to Mr. Isles and he held it in his while she thanked him for a lovely afternoon. She invited him to return and have tea with her again. He looked her in the eyes with love and tears as Miss Ginny headed down from the porch to bring Sophie inside.

On Ms. Sophie's left ring finger, she still wore her gold wedding band, as did William Ferrell Isles.

It was their sixtieth wedding anniversary.

BLACK WIDOW

When Bradley Erickson died at thirty-three from a congenital heart defect, no one cried louder at his funeral than his bride, Christina. It took four pallbearers to tear her off the casket at Forest Lawn Cemetery in Los Angeles, California. Tina and Brad had been married for one month when he met his demise.

She stood to inherit his Beverly Hills mansion and all assets, after the estate settled in one year. In California, without a prenuptial agreement, the estate was granted to the surviving spouse. Tina wore black for a year, received visitors with condolences, and remained inside.

Her hair, nails, massages, personal training, and clothing were handled in the mansion. Tina's maintenance was expensive, but Bradley's attorney, Jaime Hernandez, paid her bills that came to his office. Jaime, one of Beverly Hills's most prominent estate planning attorneys, frequently visited Tina for her deceased husband's financial matters.

One year after Bradley died, Tina changed her demure brown hair updo to frosted blonde, and let her long hair down. Widow's threads were replaced by light, breezy shifts and low-cut, sleeveless dresses. Tina spent most of her time by the pool, working on her suntan and body training, and preferred wearing white to her best advantage.

A single man, Jaime noticed Tina's change from a grieving widow to an available female, and was receptive to her. Their afternoon business meetings evolved to outdoor candlelit dinners, sometimes with an evening swim afterward. Tina had tired of waiting for the estate to be settled, and was romancing Jaime to close it soon.

Tina's feminine charm, home, and future assets appealed to Jaime, who owed alimony and child support to two ex-wives with children. As far as he knew, Tina's only relative had been Bradley. Jaime asked Tina if she would marry him, and she said she would think about it. After all, Bradley's estate had not closed.

Finally, Jaime called Tina and told her that the estate was ready to close. All she needed to do was sign a stack of documents in his office and at the bank, and Bradley's assets were hers. The next morning, she had her driver take her to Jaime's office, where she signed off on the papers, and then she proceeded to the bank.

Jaime spent the afternoon at Tiffany's, purchasing a ten-carat diamond ring for Tina, while she transferred her holdings to Switzerland. She told the housekeeping staff that she was taking a much-needed vacation, and asked them to stay and keep up the house. At five in the evening, she left on a flight to Geneva, paid for in cash.

While Tina sipped champagne in first class, Jaime received a phone call from the county coroner. At Our Lady of Angels Hospital, Bradley's X-rays had been misfiled with those of Kent Mayfield, who had died that same morning of congenital heart failure while running. The coroner asked for an exhumation of Bradley's body, since his medical records revealed that he had been in good health when he died.

Imagine Jaime's surprise when he arrived at Tina's mansion, and learned she had taken a vacation without mentioning it to anyone—not even him.

Before Tina and Bradley married, she'd worked in the records department of Our Lady of Angels Hospital, under the name of Nancy Stinger.

Tina had slipped drops of arsenic into Bradley's morning coffee, which built up a toxicity in his blood system, and killed him, just as it had her three other deceased husbands in different parts of the world.

A TOUCH OF CHIFFON

Chiffon had a penchant for lovers who worshipped her. At five foot eight, her long, platinum blonde hair, piercing light blue eyes, and shapely body turned all eyes on her every time she entered a room. Men of all ages adored her, while women detested the ground on which she walked.

As of late, Chiffon had turned her interest from the Prince of Romania to the Earl of Eastonbury, which left the prince in despair and the earl's wife in a sanitarium. Chiffon was not a woman who men simply got over. Rather, the longer apart from her, the more their desire to be with her again grew exponentially. Put simply, Chiffon was a drug that no red-blooded man was able to quit.

The Earl of Eastonbury wintered with Chiffon in her Parisian turn-of-the-century mansion in secluded ecstasy until she tired of him like the others. She had no desire to marry, and found his proposal of marriage a bore. As an heiress, she had unlimited funds at her disposal, and decided to spend the spring in Transylvania.

It was there she met an unusual count who utterly captivated Chiffon. His catlike eyes fascinated her, and the sweetness of his breath intoxicated her. She felt drawn to him because he aroused heightened sensual feelings in her like no other man had ever done before. Chiffon couldn't tear herself away from him to save her life.

Early one morning, she awoke to a bloodstained note on the white silk pillow next to her.

It read: "I've had my taste of you, darling. Your bags are packed and waiting for you downstairs. Morgwart will drive you to the train station. Good hunting, D."

SWEPT AWAY

Talia Martinez was sixteen years old and going through her first breakup. She walked alone on the beach at Carmel Bay, California where she went to think. Her first love, Eduardo, had ended their three-year relationship and asked Cindy Cardoza to go out. He wanted to see other girls, but not Talia.

While she walked, Talia envied the freedom of graceful white egrets, noisy seagulls, and red-winged blackbirds that flew away in formation. It seemed even the birds had partners and she felt more alone than ever. Tears streamed down her face as she thought about returning to high school in the fall without Eduardo by her side. Talia wished she could move away from Monterey, California and start over free from the past.

Suddenly, Talia was tossed like a rag doll into the rough and cold Pacific Ocean. The Carmel River had pushed her with its full force into the ocean, slamming her against four-foot waves and a riptide that dragged her underwater. Talia swam against the waves, but the tide dragged her farther out to sea. She gulped down salty ocean water and was tangled in strands of seaweed.

Talia was quickly losing hope when someone lifted her out of the ocean and put her down in a canoe. He turned the canoe around sideways along the waves and paddled furiously out of the ocean to the Carmel River in shallow water. Before she knew it, he had wrapped a blanket around her drenched body, which was shaking from the ice-cold sea.

The Carmel River State Beach ranger patiently explained to Talia that she had missed the danger sign near the river, which she'd crossed when it was let out to the ocean. Talia told the ranger that she was fortunate he had seen her and saved her life. She assured him that she would never cross the river again.

Talia dried herself off, thanked the ranger, waded through the shallow river water, and stepped back onto warm, coarse sand. While she walked along the shore, she thought about how close she had come to being swept away in the Pacific Ocean. She vowed that no guy would ever do that to her again.

TRAPPED

Mrs. Molly Malone, a sixty-two-year-old widow, lived in a well-manicured neighborhood on Martha's Vineyard. Her husband, who had passed on five years ago, set her up for life with his generational wealth. Michael and Molly Malone never had children, so the money was Molly's to do whatever she wanted with it.

Molly had her black, neck-length hair and red fingernails done every Wednesday at Ginger's Salon and Nail Palace. She wasn't much of a talker. Instead, she kept her ears peeled for any snippet of gossip she could pick up. Just last week, Molly had learned Mrs. Janine Harrison's youngest daughter, Layla, was getting married to Lawrence Layton, a well-to-do attorney who was twice his fiancée's age; Marilyn Meyhew, her neighbor, was stricken with her second bout of breast cancer; and last Sunday, the church she frequented had the collection money stolen. This was news for Molly to ponder.

After the beauty salon, Molly shopped at One More Time and walked out with two wrapped gifts: a sconce for Layla Harrison's wedding present and a book of poetry for Marilyn Meyhew. Molly drove straight home, called to make appointments for tea over the weekend, and laid out her clothes for the visits. Molly was so excited that she forgot to eat dinner and went to bed exhausted.

On Saturday, she arrived at the Harrison's wrapped in a large, black Persian lamb coat with an unusually large purse on her arm. She rang the doorbell and handed the wedding present to Janine after she was inside the home. Janine busily prepared scones and hot tea while Molly was in the upstairs bathroom.

Molly quietly tiptoed into Janine's bedroom, opened one dresser drawer after another, ran her right hand over and under the contents of each, pulled out a pair of long, black leather gloves, a Chanel designer silk scarf, and a magenta nightie from Rita's Secrets in the village. She slipped the items into her large purse, clasped it tightly, and walked quickly downstairs into the Harrison's parlor.

"Molly, I was starting to worry about you," Janine said. "Are you feeling all right?"

"Never better," Molly said as she settled into the sofa, eating scones and sipping hot tea.

Janine spoke enthusiastically about her daughter's wedding and her prosperous future son-in-law. Molly listened to the details with relish while she thought about the haul in her purse. Before she left, Janine showed Molly the dining room where the mahogany table was stacked with wedding presents. On her way out the door, Molly thanked Janine for the tea and said they would have to do it again soon.

The next day, Molly wore the same large coat and purse when she walked down the block to bring the ailing Marilyn Meyhew her poetry book. She and Marilyn had been neighbors for thirty years and knew each other well. Betsy, the maid, opened the door and greeted Molly.

"She's tired, but would like to see you," Betsy told Molly as she led her into the parlor. Marilyn was seated in her comfortable chair and ottoman, which Molly sat next to on the couch.

"I've been so worried about you, Marilyn, dear," Molly said. "I hope this little book of poems helps to lift your spirits," she said, handing her the book.

"I'm hanging in there, Molly. I've been through worse than this before," Marilyn said.

"I know you have, dear. You always pull through, bless your soul," Molly said. "I'm going upstairs to the powder room if you don't mind," Molly continued. "Old age doesn't suit my bladder."

Molly heard Betsy washing dishes downstairs and headed to the silver cabinet at the end of the hall. She quietly opened the top left drawer, started moving her hand inside of it, and screamed in pain. A mousetrap had snapped on the fingers of her right hand.

Betsy heard the scream and yelled from the kitchen to Molly upstairs. "Are you okay, Mrs. Malone? We've had some mice in the attic and the exterminator set some traps for them yesterday. It seems the entire village is infested. Molly?"

PASSING THROUGH

Melva was sick of the abandoned shack in Henning, Tennessee where she and Tiny had been hiding out since he pulled his last job. It had been three months since he'd robbed the local bank in Munford and he wouldn't lay a finger on the money. She was tired of heating up pork and beans, his stinking cigar smoke, and the wretched sight of his three-hundred-pound frame and sweaty bald head.

She'd had nothing to do with the robbery and he was using her to make calls from pay phones for him. After three months, Melva knew she couldn't wait another week to steal her cut before taking off. There was one saving grace in her favor—Tiny was a sound sleeper.

Melva told him that she had to get some personal items after she made his phone calls. She bought sanitary napkins and a small bottle of whiskey at the convenience store. When she returned, Tiny was busy watching the horse races on a small television. He didn't see Melva crush four sleeping pills and pour them into a glass of whiskey.

She brought Tiny his bowl of pork and beans for dinner, along with a glass of whiskey. He ate his meal while engrossed in the television, then he washed it all down with the dosed whiskey and fell asleep in his chair.

Melva reached under the bed, opened Tiny's duffle bag, and pulled out three stacks of C-notes, then she closed the bag and quietly put it back. She hid the C-notes in her bag stuffed with clothes, closed it, and left it underneath the bed.

She checked on Tiny and he was snoring. Melva put on her coat, took her bag, and slipped out the door. Three blocks away, she heard him yelling her name and ran for her life.

Pop, pop, pop!

The fool was firing his gun at her. She ducked around a corner into a diner and sat at the counter. A copper was finishing his dinner and asked if she had seen any trouble outside.

"No, sir," she said. "I'm just passing through."

"I see that," the policeman said, looking at her bag. "Odd place to pass through. The only thing that ever happened remotely close to here was a bank robbery more than three months ago."

Tiny was staggering outside the diner in the street. "Melva, I'll find you no matter where you are!" he hollered.

She threw her bag over the counter and jumped behind it.

Tiny staggered inside and the cop tackled him to the ground. Then he cuffed him and took possession of the gun.

"You can come out from behind the counter with your bag, honey," the policeman said.

She did as he instructed, and he grabbed her bag as soon as it was close enough. "Just as I thought," the copper said when he opened her bag. "The dough from the bank robbery. Honey, didn't you know those $100 bills were marked?"

BOTTLED UP

The fast curve below Savannah's two-story Victorian home in Macon, Georgia had become a magnet for privileged male adolescent drivers. At least three times a year, a sixteen-year-old driver crashed his expensive new sports car into the retaining wall below the steep hill of her home. The melee always played out the same.

Between 2:30 a.m. to 3:30 a.m., a large crash shook her home to its bones. Savannah would put on her robe, run down the hill, and be met by a broken water hydrant with explosive water spilling out into the street, and a car smashed into her decimated retaining wall. Every time, she called emergency and asked for an ambulance. Often, the Jaws of Life were required to extricate the young driver from his car. He would be helped onto a stretcher and loaded into an ambulance, which disappeared with lights flashing and siren screeching, along with the police car.

In the light of day, Savannah would return to the bottom of the hill, strewn with beer bottles and the remnants of her retaining wall in the ivy.

Then something changed. The same scene played out early one Thanksgiving morning. A young man driving his new red Corvette at one hundred and ten miles an hour had killed his best friend in the crash. When Savannah walked down to the bottom of her hill, she saw the driver's father surveying the damage.

Without a word, she took a photograph of the wreckage, plucked the beer bottles from her ivy, put them in a large garbage bag, and placed one bottle after another on top of her remaining retaining wall around the corner from the crash.

The police stopped by and took a photo of the crash site and another of the beer bottles that Savannah had found in the ivy. The driver's father drove off when he saw the police get out of their car. After years of watching the destruction of adolescent males who crashed expensive sports cars, Savannah could not keep silent a moment longer.

She had kept her anger at their alcoholic behavior bottled up far too long. It took the death of the driver's fifteen-year-old male passenger to release it.

MERRY WIDOWS

Cities are full of dead husbands who have worked themselves into early graves for insatiable wives living high on the hog. These women show off jewels on their fingers with manicured nails and under chins paid for by the sweat and sacrifice of their deceased spouses, nailed six-feet-under by cement tombstones behind black wrought iron gates. These merry widows flaunt their wealth in full-length minks and live the lives of the rich and famous on the cover of magazines.

He waits to reel in one of these payday greenbacks using flattery, handsome charms, and any number of devices at his disposal while in pursuit. He hunts on luxury cruises, at private social clubs, in opera houses, dining in A-list restaurants, attending high society weddings, and showing up at the occasional conciliatory funeral.

He has vastly enriched his bank account from the toil of these showy women's dead husbands.

An international market exists for the jewels he has collected—diamonds, emeralds, sapphires, rubies, and tanzanite. Greenbacks are also an internationally traded commodity. The merry widows soon find they have accumulated a tab to be paid for his services.

It is over quickly. He locks one hand down firmly over an agape mouth and strangles a neck with the other. His familiarity with the location of jewels and cash in their boudoir affords him the advantage of cleaning them out in under five minutes. He has a key to let himself in discreetly, and leaves as quietly as a cat.

Yes, he attends the funerals of all his widows, his merry widows. He pushes on, expanding his social circle and portfolio across the country.

He is the merry widow-maker and he hits his mark.

THE BASEBALL FIELD

Back in the 50s, Melanie's dad built a two thousand square foot, three-bedroom family home on a corner lot for twenty thousand dollars in the San Joaquin Valley, California. It was in a good neighborhood with homes that cost about the same and families who lived on the same income. The homes were as different in appearance as the people who lived in them.

Parents took turns entertaining their neighbors on Saturday evenings in their homes. Homemade ham and cheese sandwiches with the crust cut off, chips, and dip were served by their children, along with alcoholic beverages. Then card games occupied the adults for the rest of the evening. The adults knew their neighbors' children and liked them.

During the week after school, their children met in the center of their neighborhood on a baseball field of freshly mowed green grass. It was here the children greeted each other, became friends, and played baseball. The children were as different as their families.

However, the children didn't seem to notice any differences because their parents were friends. Children of Catholic, Jewish, Quaker, atheist, Portuguese, Hispanic, Japanese, Dutch, Irish, French, and immigrant parents came together on the baseball field to play ball. Boys and girls played together without incident. Their parents had not exposed their children to bigotry, nor religious or gender bias.

The day came when the youngest daughter of a Catholic family called the son of a Jewish family an anti-Semitic word that she had heard in ballet class but did not understand. Tears streamed down the young boy's face and he ran home crying. The young girl knew that she had done something terrible and left the field, along with the rest of the children.

When her father came home from work, he received a phone call from a friend who was the young boy's father. He apologized to his friend and promised that he would take care of the matter with his daughter. He angrily reprimanded his daughter and emphasized that the word she had used—and any other words she might hear in the future—were never to be used in or outside the home. While her terrified siblings watched, he vigorously washed her mouth out with soap for several minutes and sent his youngest daughter to bed without dinner.

The next morning, Melanie's dad walked his youngest daughter to the young boy's home. He stood back while she apologized to the boy and promised she would never say the name she had called him again. Both children cried and hugged. His youngest daughter and the young boy walked hand in hand to the baseball field and played ball with the other children. Melanie's dad was invited into the home for coffee by his best friend.

After the incident, Melanie's dad never had to face up to the use of a slur in his home.

STELLA'S HEAVEN

Stella Max was a streetwise dame from the wrong side of the tracks in Chicago. She was good-looking, polished, and, at thirty-seven, had clawed her way to creative director at the best advertising agency in Chi-town. Nobody was going to get between Stella and her heaven of a corner window office overlooking Lake Michigan. Anyone who tried to go after her job could pry the keys to her domain from her cold, dead fingers.

Stella was married to her job, worked weekends and holidays, and traveled on the fly. Clients liked her and respected her judgment. In the fifteen years she had been with the firm, she had climbed up the ranks by virtue of hard work and doing whatever it took to get ahead.

Dan Monihan, the agency's owner, had an eye on Stella to take over when he was ready to retire in five years. Dan had hired Stella and mentored her, proudly watching her win large accounts and take on more responsibility. Over the years, men had left the firm because they couldn't balance their work and family, but Stella had stayed the course—she was all about building the business. Stella was living proof that anything a man could do, she could do better.

Conlin and Dunlap were collecting bids on print and radio advertising for Sparklesmile toothpaste, which would be a star account to add to the Monihan Advertising agency's portfolio. "Stella, I'm sending you to Ewing, New Jersey on Monday for the presentation. I assume you can make it," Dan told her.

"Of course, Dan," Stella assured him. "I'll land that baby and bring it home."

Stella worked with her team all weekend on a top-notch presentation. She packed it up, and left from the office for O'Hare, landing in Newark at midnight. She grabbed her carry on and presentation case, and ran for a cab to her hotel, paid for by the owners of the account. By one o'clock in the morning, she was fast asleep in her hotel bed.

At eight-thirty in the morning, Stella hailed a hack and told the cabby to take her to Conlin and Dunlap in Ewing. Ten minutes before her appointment, she had registered with the receptionist and was seated in the large waiting area, presentation case in hand. Stella watched a team of six men leave when a woman came out behind them, said they were ready for her, and ushered her into a large conference room filled with twelve men.

When she entered, the men looked flabbergasted and were speechless. Stella introduced herself and shook hands with the owners, Gerald Conlin and Douglas Dunlap. Dunlap's son, Charles, also shook hands with Stella, and smiled. Stella put her presentation up on the easels at the front of the room and went through the print ad step by step. When she came to the last line of the ad, "You can have white teeth and fresh breath with Sparklesmile," the men stood up and applauded.

"There's an ad that makes sense!" Conlin exclaimed.

"We can use the last line in our radio jingle," Dunlap responded.

"Well done, Stella!" said Charles. "You are the first to put white teeth and fresh breath together for our product."

"Gentlemen, we have a winner here," Conlin said.

"I concur," Dunlap responded.

"We don't have a minute to waste. Let's take a vote. Hands up for white teeth and fresh breath with Sparklesmile!" Conlin directed.

All the male hands in the room went up.

"It's unanimous! Our print and radio advertising are now in Stella's capable hands. Charles, our Chief Financial Officer will explain the budget and financial details to you over dinner, Stella. May I be the first to congratulate you on a stellar presentation and winning our account. I am sure we will do business together for many years to come," Dunlap said.

"Here, here!" cheered the company men.

"Thank you, gentlemen," Stella responded. "It is my pleasure." Then she quickly packed up her display, shook hands with Conlin and Dunlap, and Charles walked her out of the room into the hallway.

"How would you like the juiciest steak in town?" Charles asked Stella.

"I'd love it," she answered.

"Great! I'll pick you up in the lobby of your hotel at six o'clock and we'll leave for Mason's. I'll look forward to it," Charles said with a sparkle in his eye.

"I will too," said Stella, and walked toward the elevator.

She hailed a hack back to her hotel. During the ride, Stella kept thinking about the tall, handsome, blue-eyed executive who was taking her to dinner. She noticed he was not wearing a wedding ring.

Stella paid the driver and hurried to her room to call Dan and tell him the good news. She was surprised to see a large box of candy waiting for her in the room, no card in sight. She put her portfolio case and bag down, then sat and asked to be connected to the Chicago operator. "Monihan Advertising," Stella asked the operator.

"Connecting," the operator responded.

"Hi Shirley, this is Stella. I'm calling for Dan," Stella said.

"Oh, Stella! He's been waiting to hear from you. I'll get him for you," Shirley answered.

"Stella, what's the word?" Dan asked.

"We have the account, Dan," Stella answered. "I'm meeting with Charles Dunlap this evening at dinner over the budget and financials."

"I knew you would do it! Congratulations, Stella," Dan exclaimed. "Now, here is what I want you to do. Tell Charles that you'll return with their package and I'll go over the budget and particulars here with our people. After I've reviewed and reached an agreement, he can fly to Chicago so we can sign off on the paperwork. Deal?"

"Deal," answered Stella. "Dan, when I returned to my hotel room, I noticed a box of candy without a card waiting for me. What do you think?"

"Don't go near it. The advertising business can get overly competitive, as you know. Why don't you ask the front desk who delivered it?" suggested Dan. "Oh, and Stella, don't go anywhere without your presentation case. Remember to take it to dinner with you."

"Got it," responded Stella. "I'll see you back in Chicago tomorrow afternoon."

"Thank you, Stella," Dan said. "You're one in a million."

Stella asked the reception desk if they had a record of who had delivered the large box of candy, but they did not. The maid knocked on her door to see if she needed her bed turned down and she declined. However, she asked if the maid knew anything about the candy.

The maid asked housekeeping down the hall if anyone knew about the box of candy and a man stopped vacuuming to answer. "A fella gave me a C-note to leave the candy on the desk in your room, miss," he said.

"What did he look like?" Stella asked.

"He was wearing a dark tie and suit," he said. "He must have been in his thirties. Looked like the business type."

"I wonder why he didn't leave the candy at the front desk for delivery," Stella said.

"It's against the hotel rules for housekeeping staff to bring contraband into a guest's room," Stella's maid said. "And to take one hundred dollars to do it gets you fired, mister," the maid said to the male worker. "You better get down there and tell them what happened before I do," she said.

"I'm sorry for all the trouble, miss," he said to Stella, and walked away.

"Thanks for getting to the bottom of this," Stella said to the maid, and closed the door.

Stella was downstairs in the lobby five minutes early with her purse and presentation case, waiting for Charles. She looked elegant in her black evening dress with pearl earrings and necklace and camel cashmere coat. Charles arrived on time and beamed when he saw his attractive dinner companion. Then he chuckled at her tight grip on the portfolio.

"One cannot be too careful," Stella remarked, and walked with Charles to his car.

During the drive, Stella asked him if his office had sent a large box of candy to her room and told him it had been there when she'd returned from the meeting earlier. Charles said they did not and seemed perplexed when Stella told him about the odd delivery arrangements. The whole set up sounded sketchy to him, and he said it would be wise not to touch the chocolates. Stella agreed.

Stella's angst over the chocolates dissipated during dinner over whiskey, blood-rare steak, and Charles. She found his intelligence and reassuring voice relaxing and comfortable to be with. She told him about Dan's wish to review the budget and financials himself and have Charles fly in for a final agreement and signature meeting.

"So, I'll have more of you to look forward to being with in the future," Charles said. "Cheers to us." Charles raised his glass.

"Cheers to us." Stella laughed playfully and clicked her glass with his.

As they walked outside the front of the restaurant, Charles said, "I can't remember the last time I've had such a relaxing evening. Thank you, milady." Then he gave the ticket for his car to the parking valet.

While his back was turned, a man in a black suit tried to wrestle the presentation case from Stella and dragged her down the street with it. Stella was sprawled out in the street, face down, her hands clutched to her purse and case. Charles and the parking attendants raced to lift her up out of the street before a car almost hit her.

Charles gently lifted Stella into his car and made sure her purse and case were with him. He made it to the emergency unit of the hospital in five minutes. Stella insisted he was making too much of a fuss, but he was genuinely shaken up.

After a head X-ray, the doctor said that Stella had sustained facial, palm, and leg contusions and abrasions, but no breakage, sprains, nor permanent damage. He did suggest that she should be observed for twenty-four hours. Charles told him about everything odd that had happened to Stella during her stay in New Jersey, from the box of candy delivery to the attempted theft of the presentation case and the near miss by a car outside the restaurant.

The emergency doctor brought in Detective Hodges from the hallway and they discussed the situation. The policeman smelled a rat. He sent a cop over to Stella's hotel to pick up the box of candy and have it tested. Then he told Stella that she should stay in the hospital overnight and he would post a policeman outside of her room.

Charles said he would call Dan and tell him about the incident outside the restaurant, Stella's injuries, and that she would return later than expected.

"What about my presentation case and purse?" Stella asked, concerned.

"I'll be in your room with both of them," Charles responded with the utmost concern.

Stella seemed relieved that Charles was taking charge of her case and purse. Once she was cleaned up, bandaged, and in bed, the nurse gave her a pain pill to help her sleep. She thanked Charles, who looked at her with loving concern.

He wondered how anyone could have been so dedicated they would have allowed themselves to be dragged down a street clutched to an advertising presentation case, rather than let it be stolen. He also marveled at how, in less than twenty-four hours, he was falling madly and deeply in love with Stella. Her brilliance, beauty, and bravery had conquered him.

The nurse brought Charles coffee throughout the night while Stella slept. In the morning, Detective Hodges pulled Charles into the doorway. He told Charles that the chocolates had been tested and were laced with rat poison. The hotel housekeeping worker was down at the police station working with a sketch artist on a drawing of the man in a dark suit who had paid him to put the chocolates in Stella's room. The detective said he would have a cop bring the drawing to Stella by noon to see if she recognized his face.

Stella awoke in pain and the nurse gave her another pill. Then she had her breakfast and went back to sleep. The bruising on her face was much worse and had turned black and purple. Charles smiled and put his hand over hers while she slept.

At noon, a cop arrived with a sketch of the man who had hired the housekeeping staffer to put the chocolates in Stella's room. Charles stood next to Stella while the sketch was presented. Charles stared at the likeness and was stunned.

"I saw that man!" Charles exclaimed. "He was in our conference room yesterday, pitching an ad before Stella."

Stella looked at the sketch and thought he looked familiar, but did not know him.

"I know him all right," Charles said. "His name is Garford Gravely. He is the son of Garrison Gravely of Hartford, Gravely and McDermott Advertising in New York."

"I cannot believe this," Stella said.

"We'll get him, miss," the policeman said. "He'll pay dearly for this."

"You'll want the parking attendants at Mason's Steakhouse to have a look at the sketch and see if he's the guy who tried to steal Stella's advertising presentation case," suggested Charles. "Once word gets out, their clients will start dropping like flies." He turned to Stella. "Oh, baby, I can't believe what you've been through," Charles said to Stella. "One thing I do know—now that I have found you, I don't want to be without you."

"How do you feel about moving to Chicago, Charles?" Stella asked.

Charles reached down and gave Stella a soft, loving kiss on the lips.

Stella's heaven had just expanded to embrace her love of a lifetime, Charles Dunlap.

LOVE'S GIFT

The third decade of the millennium had taken its toll on Katerina and Jacob Dickenson. A plague had swept the planet and left them both jobless. They had been forced to move into a small garage with a cold cement floor and no heat for $50 per week.

Their room came with a hot plate, on which Katerina made one meal a day to sustain them—clear broth. She also used the hot plate to boil water for instant coffee, which they drank to dull their appetite. The Dickensons had one hot water bottle between them, warmed before retiring to their large sleeping bag at nighttime.

Jacob left the frigid room early every morning to look for day jobs as a handyman. During the week, he found work cleaning rain gutters, raking leaves, trimming hedges, washing windows, and other odd jobs in nearby neighborhoods for $15 on an average day. On weekends, Jacob rarely found work because people were home to do the chores themselves. He still persevered, and stood on a corner with a cardboard sign that read, "Work Needed. Anything will help." People drove by and pretended not to see him because they thought he was homeless and wanted a handout. On a good week, Jacob brought home $100 in cash, leaving $50 to pay the electric bill, buy broth, and personal necessities.

Katerina walked block after block and looked for colorful glass vases that neighbors discarded in boxes on the curb for garbage pickup. She brought them home in a garbage bag and cleaned them up. When Katerina decided she had enough vases, she went out with a smaller bag of vases, cut winter flowers from city sidewalks, arranged them in vases and went door to door to sell them.

Her arrangements of showy, hardy red roses, flowering violet irises, sprigs of red holly with glossy green leaves, and stunning white heather in cobalt blue, ruby red, and deep green vases turned neighbors into regular customers. On a good day, she sold three vases of flowers and came home with $6.00 in cash. Katerina's hard work averaged $20 in cash per week, which she saved for emergencies.

Fortunately, Katerina and Jacob were young and in good health from walking. They were better off than many other people who had lost their jobs due to the pandemic. Most were evicted from their homes and forced to sleep overnight in freezing and dangerous public parks where they were resented by neighbors. The less fortunate risked injury and death from thugs who overtook the parks in the dark of night when they slept. At least the young couple had a roof over their heads and each other.

However, Christmas was approaching, and they agonized privately on what to give each other.

Unknown to the other, both came up with the same idea. On Saturdays, wealthy neighbors who were about to move away put items they no longer wanted on the curb for free or garbage pickup. Katerina and Jacob carefully pushed discarded silverware, full sets of expensive china, electronics, and antique furniture in grocery carts into the pawn shop for cash by 4:00 p.m. every Saturday. Jacob pushed two carts tied together with rope when he collected his treasures.

It was amazing that they never saw each other. In three weeks, each had amassed a fortune—$75 for Christmas!

Jacob thought at length about his wife's present. He despaired that she'd sold her wedding ring because he'd lost his job and the government had threatened to put him in jail if he didn't pay his taxes. Katerina's wedding ring had meant the world to her and he didn't like her being without it.

Katerina was distraught over the fact that she'd never had the money to buy her husband a wedding ring. When she saw a solid gold size-ten men's round wedding ring in the pawn shop for $30, she bargained with the owner and bought it for $25 in cash. She walked to the dollar store next door and bought $50 worth of meat, cheese, bread, and a pie for their Christmas celebration.

Katerina felt lighter than she had during the past burdensome dark year as she pushed the grocery cart filled with food and a special present for her husband, down block after block of city sidewalks. When she arrived near their garage, she spotted a card table with two matching folding chairs on the sidewalk for pickup. Katerina piled her new dining set onto the cart in delight.

Once at home, she lovingly arranged a vinyl tablecloth designed with tiny poinsettias over the table and placed a vase of holly leaves with red berries in the center. Then she carefully cut the meat and cheese into thin slices, fixed the spread with bread onto paper plates, and set them on the new dining table with plastic utensils. Finally, Katerina placed a berry pie with a holly leaf on top onto the table. She had finished making the broth when Jacob walked in.

He looked in surprise at the festive Christmas feast prepared by his wife on the table with two chairs and laughed good-naturedly. Then he reached into the right pocket of his jeans, knelt down on the garage floor next to Katerina, held up a gold box, and asked, "Will you marry me, my love?"

"Of course, Jacob," Katerina responded, and opened the box. Inside was the wedding ring she had hocked to keep her husband out of jail. Jacob firmly slipped it onto her finger while she cried tears of joy.

Katerina handed her husband a silver box and told him, "You should have had this a long time ago."

Jacob opened the box, saw a gleaming gold wedding ring, and put it on his ring finger, tears streaming down his face.

"I love you more than you will ever know," he said.

They hugged while crying together.

He went outside and brought back brown paper bags filled with meat, cheese, and bread.

The magi had gifted the Dickensons at Christmas.

A DOCTOR IN THE FAMILY

After sending five adolescents off to college, Mr. Langley was elated to have one of them finish medical school. The other four had excuses for not earning their advanced degrees: not completing a thesis, not completing an oral exam, dropping out to backpack in Europe, and an unplanned pregnancy. However, the youngest son in the Langley tribe was the first to make his father proud.

Mr. Langley boasted to his family and friends that his son, Hunter, was returning home to work as a doctor. He arranged a welcome home dinner for his son in honor of his monumental achievement. "I hear you put in a great deal of time to become a doctor," Mr. Ross said to Hunter at the dinner.

"Yes, sir. Four years in pre-med. Then four years in medical school. Finally, three years in residency," Hunter said.

"That's great, son," said Mr. Langley pridefully, his arm around his son. "Are you going to be a cardiologist or neurologist at County Hospital?"

"Actually, I'm the new coroner at the County Morgue," Hunter replied.

Quietly, Mr. Langley muttered, "I'm going to wash my hands," and quickly exited the room.

PIERCE COLLINS BARTLETT

Inside the New Horizons Hospital in Boca Raton, Florida, Pierce Collins Bartlett, a real estate developer and staunch member of the community, lay in a coma. He was hooked up to monitors for his heart rate, blood pressure, and vitals, and another machine that kept him breathing. No one could figure out why the healthy fifty-year-old male had collapsed suddenly and failed to regain consciousness.

A tearful fifty-something woman with short, frosted blonde hair and two adult children in tow entered the room. They seated themselves on either side of the bed, holding his hands. "Oh, my dear, please wake up. If not only for myself, awaken for your children. Their college tuition is due, the bank keeps calling about the mortgage being behind three months, and I don't know anything about our financial situation," pleaded Myrna, his wife.

After sitting next to Pierce and complaining for half an hour without a response, Myrna and the children left his room quietly.

At 9:00 in the evening when visitation ended, a twenty-seven-year-old pregnant Cuban woman pleaded with the nurse to let her in to see her husband. The woman held a sleeping baby in her arms, and the nurse walked her down to his room and opened the door, then closed it. She sat down in a chair next to her husband, placed the sleeping baby beside him on the bed, and gently held his hand.

"Please come back to me. Please, my husband. I love you more than words can say. Your children need you as much as I do. How can I raise them without their father?" she asked with a tear-stained face. Leticia told Pierce how much he was loved, and left when the nurse told her it was time to go.

Pierce never came out of his coma. Imagine Myrna's surprise when she learned that her marriage to Mr. Bartlett was not legal because he was already married to a third wife, Hizenia, who had Alzheimer's and would be provided for the rest of her life in a nursing home. However, he had divided the remainder of his assets between her and Leticia.

The coroner never found the cause of Mr. Bartlett's coma. It was Myrna who had crushed a seed from the Cerbera odollam tree in his morning coffee after she had seen him kiss Leticia and her infant son through the window of The Little Folk's clothing store the day before.

DIRTY LAUNDRY

Loretta Reynolds enjoyed attending church on Sundays in the small seaside village of Morro Bay, California where she had lived her entire life. She savored the sense of community and sharing love with her family, friends, and other church members. The uplifting feeling that she experienced by going to church sustained her during the week. When her boyfriend, Henry, asked her to join him at his family's church an hour away in the country, she agreed and looked forward to it.

Loretta parked her car in a dirt lot, hurried into the packed church, and sat next to Henry, who had snagged seats in a pew right in front of the pulpit. Loretta felt pretty in her new flowery spring dress and white pearl necklace from her grandmother.

A woman wearing a stern expression stood at the pulpit.

She spoke at length of her shame for driving a speedboat under the influence twenty years prior, at the age of seventeen. Her best friend had been water skiing when she'd lost control of the boat, which had gone faster and faster, and had whipped the water skier into a wooden pier. The speaker had walked away without any serious injury, but her friend had been paralyzed from the waist down for the rest of her life.

Her speech brimmed over with years of guilt and self-loathing. The negativity emanating from the speech gave Loretta knots in her stomach, and she folded her arms. She tuned out and began to pray for the woman.

Next, a man stood up from his seat and proclaimed, "I cheated on my wife last week." He sat down, stood up again, and added, "Twice."

Another man popped up and announced, "I beat my wife again last week."

A well-dressed woman in a suit slowly got up and said, "I stole from the petty cash drawer at work and bought a new purse to match my pumps."

Loretta's neck was stiff, jerking it quickly from one person to the next during the airing of their dirty deeds. Finally, she lowered her head and couldn't listen anymore. She didn't understand why the members who had stood up and stated their misdeeds had not handled their business at home.

After the service, Henry admitted to Loretta that he was seeing two other women.

Loretta said she was going home to do her own dirty laundry, and never saw him again.

HER BEST ASSETS

Flora walked out of the opera house into the fresh night air. She stepped off the curb to cross the street, thinking about picking up her parked car, and making the short drive home to her Boston brownstone. In the middle of crossing the street, she felt a sharp pointed object between her shoulder blades.

"Keep moving, lady, or you'll get it in the back," a deep, rough voice said. He pushed her along quickly to the other side of the street.

Flora felt the dampness of her silk wrap around her little black dress and stopped to look down. Droplets of blood dripped from the back of her to the ground. She figured the man with the weapon must have been injured.

He pushed her forward again while people watched with concern on the sidewalk.

He was breathing heavy when she extended her long right leg backward and brought his right leg down with her spiked silver high heel shoe. He slipped on the wet cement and landed flat on his back. During his fall, his knife flew down the sidewalk, and was picked up by a security guard standing among the bystanders.

The guard held a gun on the man, tied his hands behind his back, and seated him on the sidewalk. When the ambulance and police arrived, they asked Flora how she had managed to subdue the criminal who had been in a convenience store robbery earlier in the evening.

"My late husband, Andrew, always said my long legs were my best assets. I used them to trip him," Flora said proudly.

SHADE

Letty's eyes darted frantically, searching for shade of night—anywhere she could hide from her boss, Mrs. Woods. She had called in sick and was supposed to be at home in bed with a fever of one hundred and two. When Letty spotted a dark alley, she rushed around a corner, pulled the collar of her raincoat up, and hid behind a dumpster.

She heard Mrs. Woods haranguing her husband all the way down the street and could empathize. It was hard to have a boss who found fault with her at work and put her through the ringer day after day. She couldn't imagine what kind of a nightmare Mrs. Woods must be as a wife.

Once the voice was out of range, Letty rushed out of the alley and continued down the block to an apartment building. She rang the buzzer of number thirty-two and the front door of the building opened. She hurried up three flights of stairs and found the door open.

Letty took a tablespoon from the kitchen and put it on the table next to the bedside of her father, Jimmy. She had taken the day off to tend to his cough and fever. She pulled the bottle of cough syrup out of a bag and poured it into the tablespoon for him.

"Here, Daddy, please drink all of this up. The pharmacist said it will make you feel better," she said.

Jimmy started coughing badly. When he stopped, he said, "Thank you, baby girl. I don't know what I'd do without you." He took his time and slowly sipped the entire tablespoon of cough syrup.

"The syrup should make you sleep better too," Letty said, and wiped the sweat from his forehead.

"Anna May will be checking on you through the night and tomorrow while I'm at work," Letty said. "Be sure and tell her if you need anything and I'll go to the store on the way over."

Jimmy smiled lovingly at his only daughter. "Thank you, baby. I love you with all of my heart."

"I love you too, Daddy," Letty said. "Get some shut-eye and I'll see you tomorrow night." Letty quietly let herself out and locked the door.

Letty walked two blocks and hailed a cab.

"Please take me to midtown at 5th and Powell Street," she told the driver.

Inside her apartment building, she took an elevator up to the fifth floor. She opened the door and her husband helped remove her coat and kissed her.

"Sweetheart, you are working too hard," he said. "Let me draw you a bath."

"Thank you, dear," Letty responded. "A bath and a good night's rest sure sound good."

Letty sat in front of her dressing table mirror and noticed the shadows under her light brown eyes. Her skin was pallid, probably from the stress of worrying about her dad. He'd had her late in life, and had raised her as a single man after her mother had left.

"Honey, your bubble bath is ready," said her husband. He did not know about Jimmy.

It was 1942 in Philly and Letty was passing as a white woman.

OWL MAN

A forty-two-year-old, bald, round-faced, large brown-eyed, horn-rimmed spectacled neighbor of five feet, four inches had a penchant for peeping in his neighbors' windows. His single, petite, blonde next-door neighbor named him "Owl Man," because he had peeped in her large floor-to-ceiling windows several times as she looked out at the water in Holland, Michigan. When caught in the act, he scurried away like a rat jumping ship.

Owl Man was married with an infant son, yet his family was not enough to keep him from his hobby. One summer, he concocted the perfect excuse to peep on his blonde female neighbor—replacing the termite-infested wood inside the low stucco wall marking off his property. The wall was four feet high and gave him a perfect view over it into her dining room and kitchen.

It ran the full length of his home. After he removed the infested wood, he sawed new wood and nailed it inside, section by section. Each time he worked on it, he removed the wooden top piece and replaced it when finished for the day.

This project broadened his peeping turf to his female neighbor's recycled water fountain, which started around the corner from the wall and extended twelve feet down to the lake. The fountain gave him a bird's-eye view downhill of her outdoor shower, dock, and boat, which was often occupied by his neighbor and her friends. That summer, she had one new male friend who kept her busy in the boat and her home.

While he worked, Owl Man saw the couple kayak, fish, and canoodle in the boat. He also watched them eat dinner in the dining room, which was about five feet from her fountain. He became more interested in the romance with her new man than the repair work.

One Saturday night, the blonde and her beau were enjoying a romantic candlelit dinner, but it was too dark for Owl Man to peep. He moved onto her deck for a better view.

Suddenly, an animal with long claws jumped on his back and he fell backward onto the wood deck. Owl Man shrieked as a family of raccoons who were living inside a barbecue on the deck pinned him to the wood planks. His horn-rimmed glasses fell off in the melee and he couldn't fend off the wild raccoons.

His neighbor's male friend flicked a switch from the wall inside, which turned on an outside spotlight on the deck. Owl Man's wife walked out from the back of their home to see what had happened. Her husband was still screaming wildly from the claws of the raccoons.

Owl Man's wife stood in front of the deck and saw her husband sprawled out with a pair of binoculars around his neck. The family of three raccoons were sitting alongside him in judgment of his perverted behavior.

"There are termites coming out of our wall that you were supposed to repair three months ago. Did you use termite-treated wood?" his wife asked, her arms crossed.

NOT ANYMORE

He was a pockmarked, vile-looking rodent in a two-bit suit who entered Trader Vic's with a twenty-carat blonde on his arm. What was a scar-faced rat who had crawled out of a storm drain doing with a San Francisco social debutante? He had a grip on her like a vise as he led her by his stubby arm to their red leather booth.

"We'll have two zombies, crab rangoon, crispy prawns, and cheese balls," he ordered the waiter before seeing a menu. "Then two barbecued squabs, pake noodles, and spinach for each of us will do," he said. "And keep the zombies coming, buddy," he yelled after the waiter left.

The blonde pinned a large white gardenia from the maître d' to the shoulder of her sequined gown. He moved in closer and took a whiff of the flower up to her ear. "You smell good—really good, baby," he said, and licked the inside of her ear.

Her eyes barely flinched. However, she maintained a static smile that didn't budge. All eyes in the Bongo Bongo Room were on the dame in the silver, shimmering gown with platinum blonde hair and the nasty little rat man who wouldn't keep his paws off her. Drinks were served and she took a long, refreshing sip from a straw while locking eyes with a tall, handsome, well-dressed man dining alone across the room.

The appetizers and entrees arrived at the same time, which put Scarface in a sour mood. When he was asked if everything was all right, he scowled at the waiter and tore the squab apart with his bare hands. His dining companion ate a cheese ball and took another sip of her zombie. The waiter replaced the depleted zombies with fresh drinks.

The Polynesian decor and music in the dining room provided a festive environment enjoyed by all its patrons, except the nasty man. For a small man, he had a large appetite. He had devoured all the food on his plate, most of the hors d'oeuvres, and asked the woman if he could have her squab since she hadn't touched it. She pushed her plate over to him. Dining with him would have made anyone lose their appetite.

Grease from the barbecued squab dripped from his fingers and chin. The blonde bombshell continued to stare into the eyes of the attractive man dining alone. Diners around their booth stared at the little man as he slurped and grunted while eating his dinner.

The waiter removed empty plates and brought hot wet towels for them to clean their hands. The rat man wiped off his face and hands with them. He downed his drink and asked the waiter for the bill. While he paid, the woman went to the ladies' room.

Scarface waited for her outside the room and took her by the arm out of the restaurant into the parking lot. Three flashes of white light flew from a car driving by and hit the rat man in the midsection. He collapsed against the restaurant, down to the parking lot asphalt. The blonde screamed as he bled out from the belly.

The parking lot attendants gathered around him and called an ambulance. Red flashing lights atop police cars with sirens screeching roared into the parking lot. A detective rushed to the little man to take his pulse, but there was none.

"Isn't that Mickey, the gambling rat?" he asked.

"Yes, that was him," answered the blonde-haired woman.

"He owned contracts on most of the poor suckers in Frisco," the detective said. "Lookee here. Even the rat man's head is under a storm drain. Do you gamble, miss?" asked the detective.

"Not anymore," the woman answered.

NO GOOD DEED

Shelley Simpson inspected the Lake Dryhole area every night during her evening walk. She fortified herself with a pair of binoculars and a camera to take photographic evidence. Shelley was on a mission to make all of her neighbors comply with the rules of her homeowners association—whether they belonged to it or not.

Dog poop left on the grass of the city sidewalk? Children skateboarding in the middle of the street? A car that she had not seen before parked on the street? Shelley could always be counted on for a photo of the address and evidence.

Mrs. Simpson's photos and accusations increasingly annoyed the readers of their local online news digest, but no one said a word. They feared the neighborhood watcher would appear on their property next with her dreaded camera pointed at them. Most ignored her accusations.

One evening, Shelley walked the full twenty blocks without finding a blade of grass disturbed, until she came upon a broken sprinkler leaking water from the sidewalk into the gutter and street. Taking a wide stance for a shot of the corner sprinkler, a skateboarder zoomed around her on the sidewalk, and she lost her footing. Shelley slipped and fell backward, dropping her camera onto the hard, wet cement.

Lying on the wet cement, she was seething with anger. After walking twenty blocks, she had her chance and lost it. She used her hands to help herself stand up, bent over to grab her camera, and was still wearing her binoculars around her neck. Fortunately, her camera wasn't broken.

She took another look at the faulty sprinkler and swore under her breath. It was off.

CHANEL

Chanel heard her beloved mama's voice beating in the rags and bone of her heart: "Girl, you don't have to run with every no-account boy just to make do. No decent churchgoing man is gonna want a female with a bad reputation. Besides all that, you could end up pregnant and I don't have a dollah for one more mouth to feed. Ya feel me, Chanel?"

Dixon Montaigne, the insurance agency manager, gave his secretary, twenty-five-year-old Chanel, an itch she couldn't scratch. Chanel's low-cut silk blouses, tight skirts, and spiked high heels showed off her shapely breasts and long, lean legs to their best advantage. Although married for two years, Dixon could not stop Chanel from invading his thoughts all day long.

Her full lips, perfect white teeth, and soft, low, sexy voice begged him to lock the door to his office and kiss her without stopping. In his daydreams, Dixon never stopped making love to Chanel. If only she could read his mind.

However, he had married an average woman whose father owned the insurance agency. Together, they owned a gorgeous home in a well-to-do neighborhood, his-and-hers BMWs, and a fat portfolio of stocks, bonds, and liquid assets. His wife, Lilith, maintained a position on the board of their country club, ran a spotless home like clockwork, and was a gourmet cook. A fellow without a college education from the wrong side of the tracks in Selma, Alabama could have done a lot worse.

Dixon decided to keep his relationship with Chanel strictly business and pushed his thoughts of straying aside by running before and after work. It just so happened that Lilith decided to have the company Christmas party at the country club overlooking a lake. She worked with Chanel on the invitations, decorations, menu, and particulars at the club.

It was a black-tie affair with a mix of office employees, top salespeople and clients, and members on the company board of directors. Chanel's long, black designer gown received compliments from men as well as women. Imagine Dixon's surprise when Lilith's father, Edward, raised a toast to thank his daughter, and his fiancée, Chanel, for planning a successful celebration.

Chanel's mama had prepared well the rags and bone of her daughter's heart.

Made in the USA
Middletown, DE
08 May 2021

39277529R00097